# UNIVERSING

TREY PERSONS

# DEDICATION

I dedicate this book to my friends and family and all those who believed in me. Special thanks to my mom for helping me wrangle my two sons and to my dad for helping me believe in myself. This book is also for you reading this right now. Thank you for your support and never exchange your dream for the nine to five.

~Trey Persons~

# PROLOGUE

I could see the life being drained away from her as the hours went on. The nurse would come in to check on her from time to time and say her condition is still the same as it has been for the last couple of days, but I knew the truth. Some unknown illness was eating away at my wife, Krista, and no doctor, both foreign and domestic, could tell me what was happening to her. One day she's smiling at me from across the dining room table; then the next, she's found unconscious on the carpet on the living room floor. Krista is only thirty-eight, and she lived a great life as a teacher. Sharing her light with the youth of the next generation and teaching them not only how atoms are formed, but how every life is special. Sitting here, staring at her as she sleeps, I start to figure out the meaning to all her words. I must admit, I never truly thought about what she said because I was just mesmerized by her green eyes and how they go perfectly against her tanned skin. I listened to what she said just enough to respond correctly, but a part of me always just admire her energy so much that I just couldn't focus on the words coming out from behind those perfect lips. However, I can now see that energy beginning to fade. I could see her fighting to hold on to it just as a candle's wick fights to stay lit. Tears start to form in my eyes, and I take her hand, hoping she wakes up.

"What will I do without you?" I whisper to her. I can hear the door open behind me as the light from the bright hospital hallways spills into the room. The nurse just left not even an hour ago, so this could only be one other person.

"I'm back, dad." My ten-year-old son, Alec, says as he enters the room as quietly as a ten-year-old can. "The cafeteria here was out of chocolate ice-cream, so I brought you back a cup of vanilla." Alec starts to go on about how food isn't allowed out of the cafeteria while I wipe my eyes and get myself together. I haven't told him what the hands of fate have in store for his mother, yet. I want him to hold on to this peacefulness as long as he can. He hands me the cup of ice-

i

cream, and I smile gratefully.

"Thanks, Alec. I'm not surprised they didn't catch you. You're my son after all. You got all your covert operating genes from me," I say proudly. I could see the gears in his head start to turn. You could see the resemblance to his mother when he thinks. Not in his face but in his actions. They have the same gestures.

"Mom did say you were sneaky, but she knew all your moves. She told me you tried to sneak out of the delivery room when I was born, but she had Uncle Kyle outside the room."

"She told you that?" I say with a hint of surprise. "Did she tell you that Uncle Kyle fainted shortly after he escorted me back into the room?" He shakes his head. Of course, she leaves that part out. Well-" my iPhone starts to vibrate in my pocket, and as I reach for it, I remember I set an alarm for this time. A faint memory of what the newscaster said earlier today begins to rise to the surface.

"It's eight o'clock, dad! We should be able to see the shooting stars right about now!" Alec says loudly. I put my finger to my lips to calm him down as I whisper to him.

"I got the janitor to walk us out to the roof so we can see them above the lights of the city. That way, we won't miss a thing." Alec makes an exciting yelp sound as I shuffle him through the door and to the elevator.

It's unusually humid tonight as we watch the stars, waiting to see something adrift. Over my shoulder, I see the janitor at the door of the rooftop as he smokes his cigarette. I owe him another twenty dollars for getting us up here. A younger, more careless me, would've found another way to do this, but this is the best way without setting a bad example for Alec. It's quiet up here. I was expecting to hear some hustle and bustle from the streets below, but Durham, North Carolina is no metropolis. In fact, the hospital is one of the tallest buildings in the city. I also must consider that the city streets are almost barren by 8 pm.

"Has mom been awake since I went to dinner?" he asked me without taking his eyes off the night sky.

"No, son. She needed her rest while the medication the doctors gave her took its course. Maybe she will be awake in the morning when we come to visit her. I wouldn't worry too much, Alec. I know it's been a long couple of days out here at the hospital every day, but things will start looking up for us again." I lied to him. I just wasn't ready to tell him the truth. I look down at his face and could see tears running down his cheeks. He wasn't buying my story at all. Alec suddenly turns his head, and his eyes light up. I look up at the sky to see what caught his eye and there are several shooting stars. Most of them are gone in the blink of an eye, but there is this one lone star that twinkles and shines more than the others. It's traveling slower than any other shooting star I've ever seen before. Alec jumps up to his feet in amazement.

"Well, don't just stand there, Alec," I say to him excited. "Make a wish." He nods and places both his hands together. I could see his mouth move, but I can't make out what he is saying. He opens his eyes and dries his face and looks up at me.

"What did you wish for?" I ask him.

"It won't come true if I tell you, dad. Any wisher knows that."

We smile at each other and start our walk back inside. I pull the money I owe the janitor out of my pocket and slip it to him as we walk back into the stairwell.

***

The bar isn't normally this dead on a Thursday night, but tonight is an exception. My shift is nowhere near an end and time is moving slower than a snail stuck in jelly. At least I had some good company though. My regulars always keep me on my toes, and they always tip with the utmost respect for someone who's been bartending as long as I have. I begin to wipe down the countertop of the bar just as the entrance screen door flings open and in comes one of the biggest men I have ever seen. You tell a lot about a person with the way they walk, and his stride was one I've never seen before. He has a well-trimmed beard and mustache but no hair on his head. He walks over to the counter and takes a seat at one of the stools with no one on his left or right. I can see the regulars staring at him, shaken by his broad appearance. Even so, I make my way over to him without a drop of fear in my body. Everyone needs something from the bartender in the bar, no matter who you are.

"Welcome to the best bar in the South. What ya drinking tonight, big guy?" I ask him.

"I'll take a glass of any whiskey you have available with a slice of lime, sir." His voice is deep and carries heavy bass. I thought I felt the countertop vibrate as he spoke. That couldn't be the case, no. Probably just these old bones trembling.

"Coming right up and should I start a tab for you, or will this be the only drink you'll be having tonight?"

"Keep it open. The name is Felix."

"That'll get your tab started, and I'll be your bartender tonight. You can call me, Sonny. One whiskey with a lime coming right up, Felix" I walk over to the half a bottle of whiskey, grab one of the clean glasses off the countertop below the bar, and begin to dump some ice into it. I never heard someone order whiskey with lime before. It's an unusual combination of flavors, but I'm not going to question this titan man. I should probably stick with the typical bar banter to get him tipping just like I want.

"So, where ya from, Felix? Haven't seen you around here before and I've been working here for over twenty-five years," I ask as I slide his drink to him with the lime wedge on top of the glass. He takes the lime off and squeezes it into the glass of whiskey before dropping the whole thing into it.

"I've been here longer than most, but no, I'm not from this town, Sonny. No doubt about that. I wouldn't be here if it weren't for some…affairs for work that I need to take care of," Felix says as he takes a swig of his drink. "I haven't been in this part of the US in…I don't know how long."

"You look like you're from California or maybe Hawaii judging by your skin tone. I was stationed out there in my Army days. Being as big as you are, I wouldn't be surprised if you had some Samoan blood in ya somewhere." I laugh, and he grins. Hopefully, he's a good-spirited guy and doesn't mind me stereotyping him. Otherwise, my head could be found at the other end of the bar, detached from my body in one smooth punching motion. His hands were maybe a few inches smaller than cinderblocks.

"Something like that," Felix says and takes a quick look around the bar as he brings his glass up to his lips again. I follow his eyes and notice everyone was looking at him before he began his scan of the venue. I've been doing this too long not to be able to notice the ole "I don't want them to catch me staring" routine.

"What kind of work do ya do, big guy?" I ask. He pauses to think for a minute and shrugs his shoulders.

"I'm here because there will be some changes in the astrology in the area because of the recent rainfall or what you refer to as meteor showers."

"So you're some kind of scientist?" I pass him his next drink, giving him the signal to finish that one-off. He does and takes the new glass.

Look at me, Sonny. I'm no scientist," Felix says as he looks down at his gray t-shirt and blue jeans. He squeezes the juice from the lime into the whiskey and puts the lime wedge in his mouth. He drinks the whole glass of whiskey and places it delicately on the counter as if to stop himself from breaking anything. "Sonny, I'm the one that keeps this world as normal as it's supposed to be. I'm the one that keeps all the foreigners at bay. I'm here to keep anyone and anything from slipping into this one-sided realm of ours. Some of them can fly by here, and they are out of my reach, but the ones that come here, well, those are the ones that matter."

I wait for him to do two things: explain what he meant and to spit out that lime wedge.

"My job is to find the nearest bar during a region's star fall and make

v

sure no soul has drifted off course. Some of them are happy with traveling through time and space and are content being away from here, never returning. Others want to bend the laws of physics and other sciences of Earth. Most don't even get into the atmosphere, but occasionally they do."

He ain't much of a drinker. His ramble about realms, spirits, and star falls is shit I never heard of or thought about, but who am I to tell him otherwise? If I keep up the charade, I'm sure he'll tip just as good as any other drunk. I smile and say, "What happens to the ones that make it into the atmosphere?"

"Then I get rid of them before their selfish small-minded ways get the best of them and they attempt to reconnect soul with the body. We've had one god too many walk on Earth already and…"

Felix suddenly stops mid-statement and turns to the entrance of the door. The giant stands up and walks outside, looking up at the stars as he does. I look at all the other patrons, and they too are watching the front door before their eyes settle on me.

I shrug and make my way to the screen door. By this time, Felix was kneeling with a hand on the ground. For a second, I can see a faint glow radiate from him as he was kneeling, but it couldn't have been. Must have been these old eyes playing tricks on me again. The bear-like man stood upright, and it made me wonder how he even fit in the door of the bar, to begin with. He's monstrous. He looks up into the night sky and shakes his head, releasing a breath.

"A wish worth coming true is a wish worth dying for, Sonny. That's how the stars see it," says Felix as he dusts off his hands and puts them into his pockets. "I have to be going now, bartender. Thank you for the drinks. I'm not sure how much I owe you, but here is a fifty-dollar bill and keep what's left for yourself."

I walk outside and take the bill out of his hand. It looks new like it was just printed this morning. Everyone loves crispy bills. "Thank ya much, Felix. Come back here anytime ya like, big guy. The first one will be on me." He nods as he walks off into the darkness; not the darkness of the dimly lit parking lot, but the field next to it. Some people with rigs park there from time to time, but there is nothing else out there, except his silhouette. A green flash of light and a burst of wind whistles by and I could see nothing of Felix anymore. I feel the money in my hand before making my way back inside, to make sure at least this is real. I think I'm closing the joint early. My old mind can only take so much for one night.

# 1.

I fucking hate attics. They're always just the right combination of too small, too hot, or too cold. I must have been something bothersome in a past life. Wait a minute; my entire life before this calls for some large amounts of punishment and humility. Walking away from what I used to do to be a cable guy is more punishment for my generation and the next. I guess it's best to get my head out of my ass and keep looking for the main splitter. This is my last job of the day, and I need to get this one right because I've been crawling through this catacomb of an attic for far too long. I don't want to come back here and deal with this all over again.

My flashlight hits all angles of the attic, and finally, I see the main split. The main split is the splitter that all the rooms are connected to that are getting channels. If the room isn't connected, like in this case, it's not getting service. Lucky for me, a port on the splitter is open and available, so I just screw in the necessary line, and that should have that fourth TV up and running.

"That should do the trick. Now to get the hell out of here and get a beer." I carefully make my way through the attic, only letting my feet touch the rafters. I never thought about what a house was made of until I got to see what I see every day for ten to twelve hours a day. It's the life I must live now. Life is fucking funny that way. One day you're out on the streets, making powerful people more powerful, and the next, you're out saving the cable world, one house at a time. I've finally reached the entrance to the attic, and I take ease to lower myself back down to my ladder without injury or damage to the customer's personal property. Once at the bottom of the ladder, I could see the man of the house looking at me with a smile from the room that needed servicing.

"I don't know what you did up there, but everything seems to be working now. I even checked the other televisions, and they still work just as before. Thanks for your help, Mister..." He trails off, waiting for me to take the lead and tell him my name.

"I'm employee number 74809," I say as I fold up the ladder. I didn't intend to tell him anything more, but I guess not giving him an actual name would look bad when the automated survey questions them about my attitude. I can save myself another thirty-minute conversation with my boss. "I apologize. That's what the company tracts me as, but my actual name is Sean."

"Pleasure to meet you, Sean, and thanks again for hooking up the spare bedroom TV," he says as I walk down his hallway and out of his front door. "I'll be sure to have something kind to say if anyone calls, inquiring about your service to my family and me."

I place the ladder back on the van and open the side door to secure my tool bag inside it. I let out a sigh before putting my face back on and smiling at him. "I appreciate it. You have yourselves a great night and call us again if you have any questions or concerns." He waves at me. I give him a nod, jump in the van and start her up. I notice how late it is, but it'll look good on an overtime check. I'm off for the next few days so I plan to get plastered and stream a series or two. I grab my smartphone and order up a pizza before I get home. Working the past couple of days from sunup to sundown hasn't given me a lot of time to go grocery shopping. Speaking of which, I'll give the ole lady a call right now.

The phone rings and my lady sings. "You got some nerve calling here this late, Sean. You know Jada is on her way to bed now, and I don't need you calling to get her all hyped up," she says as I smile, just happy that she picked up the phone at all.

"Don't have such an attitude tonight, Jasmine. That's no way to talk to your husband." I wait for her to make the correction she always does when I try to ease myself back into her life.

"Soon to be ex-husband, Sean, and I don't know how many times I'm going have to tell you this before you get it through your head. Did you take too many blows to the face when we were living in Nashville or what?" she asks, annoyed by my positivity. She'll do anything to off-center me and say anything to remind herself why she's so mad at me.

"Baby, I could take a bat to the back of my head again and never forget how I feel about you." I could hear her take a breath and smile. I've known her since we were teenagers over fourteen years ago, so I could almost feel her every move as if it was my own.

"What are you calling for, Sean. Get to the point because I have to get our daughter to bed."

"Listen, Jazz. I'm-"

"Don't call me that anymore, Sean. You lost that right after I caught you with that whore," she demands.

"Jasmine, please, I'm not calling to fight. I just wanted to hear your voice and ask if I could come see Jada tomorrow." All I heard was silence and some shuffling of objects in the background.

"Hold on," she says before putting me on hold for another call. One could only wonder who was calling a pretty woman like her so late when I get the sinking feeling I answered my own question. That thought of realization brings me back to reality where I notice I've been stuck in a traffic jam for far too long, and if I were planning to get home before my pizza got there, I'd have to come up with a better route. Coming out here to the sticks to work sucks, but at least there was always another back road to get you where you wanted to go. I just have to avoid hitting any deer in the process.

"Alright, Sean. You can come see her tomorrow." Jasmine comes back on the line knowing she was going to find me waiting patiently. "Just call me in the morning so we can get things hashed out with the times." She sounded way to calm and nice now. The conversation she had on the phone with the mystery person must have brightened her mood, but fuck her good mood.

"Who was that on the other line, Jasmine?"

"What? You don't have the right to question me about anything

3

anymore. You didn't seem to care who was at home when you were out in the streets doing whatever."

"Who the fuck was that, Jazz? I'll find him and rip his head off so help me-"

"That's your damn problem! You don't know when to quit with all the violence and fighting. Do you think I'm gonna sit my pretty ass at home while you were out screwing that hussy while we were together? Do you think…" I meant to interrupt her while she was talking, but a sudden burst of light and flames straight ahead of the dirt road I was driving on caught my attention. The shock waves of the explosion rattles my van. Jasmine is no longer yelling at me anymore, but that's only because my phone doesn't have a signal.

I drive up to see flames across the dirt road that reminded me of a time-traveling DeLorean. I stop my van and consider my options. My life is in shambles. My wife hates my guts. I only get to see my daughter every so often and to top it all off, I'm a damn cable guy. Could things get any fucking worse?

# 2.

This is probably one of the most irrational things I've done lately. Somehow, I manage to be the only one on this road just in time to witness some kind of falling phenomenon in the darkness of the night. Maybe what I find will leave me with some cool powers or maybe it will eat my flesh alive and wear my skin around town to blend in with the rest of the world. What am I thinking? No one seems to blend in anymore these days.

Making my way through the brush and bramble off-road isn't as difficult as I thought it was going to be. Whatever it was that came through here so fast, parted its way through the forest. It made some pretty good distance away from the road. I've been walking a few steps shy of a quarter-mile. The flame streaks the object left comes to a stop a couple of strides ahead. I turn off my flashlight as I approach the scene because I notice that whatever landed back there was producing its light, but it was natural light, a soft light, similar to what a full moon would make on a cloudless night, but coming from behind the cover of the woods.

"Well, I came this far, and I can't turn back now without knowing what's back there." I sit my flashlight down next to my foot, part the bushes concealing me with both hands, only to see a pale, slightly naked woman. She's just standing there, looking at her surroundings as if she has never seen anything like it before. Maybe she was getting her bearings. Her slim frame was covered from her shoulders to the top of her knees by some sort of dark-colored cloth poncho with the hood on the back. The rest of her body is bare. She starts to examine her hands as if they weren't her own. As I look at her, I start to realize that her skin isn't pale, but the light that radiates from her is. She's some type of supercharged woman girl alien thing, and I'm not sure I want to stick around and see where this goes. Just as I think that her eyes dart over to me.

"Oh shit." She spotted me. At this point, I have ruined what little chances I had of escaping this thing, unnoticed. My dad wasn't much of a dad to me, considering the beatings and whatnot, but he didn't raise no fucking coward. She looks at me without an expression on her face as something forms and opens in the center of her forehead. She takes her hand and removes some hair away from it. It was another eye. I'm no coward, but I'm no fool either. My legs feel weightless as I run back down the path I took to get here.

There it is. I could see my van parked and waiting for me to jump back in. I manage to cover that quarter-mile probably faster than some professional football players would. I slow my pace to catch my breath and grab my keys out of my pocket as quick as I can. The movement was too quick and I fumble them. The keys hit the ground. I bend down to grab them, but when I stand upright, she is standing next to the van, holding my flashlight that I didn't think to grab before I hauled ass.

"You do not have to be afraid of me. I'm not here to hurt you or anything for that matter," she says while holding the flashlight with both hands.

Her third eye was gone without so much of a trace of anything being there. Maybe the excitement of meeting a spacewoman got the best of my imagination.

"Alright, good to know," I respond as I take a few steps back from her. Outrunning her now is not an option. My only hope was to get to my van, but she isn't going to make this easy for me. "How the hell did you beat me here?"

"I did not beat you here. I'm simply just here," she says as she tilts her head at me. "It is true what I have learned about being human over the years; you perceive time alongside distance, something that constantly moves, but you do not relate it to fate."

This can't be fucking happening. She speaks in riddles and refers to me as just human. If that wasn't a dead giveaway, she still managed to get here before I did.

"What?" I say as I grab the flashlight from her hand. "You know what, don't answer that. I have to get home before my dinner arrives, so if you can just excuse me," I say as I make my way around the front of the van. My power to ignore people has grown strong over the years, so getting in the van without so much as a look back at her was easy. I push the keys into the ignition and start the van up, then I hear the passenger door close. She is seating there, glowing softly, looking at me with those crystal blue eyes. The more I look into her eyes, the more colors I can see in them. It's like looking into a prism as the sunlight passes through it. My mouth opens, but no words come out. She turns her eyes away from mine and examines the inside of the cab with a curious expression.

"I cannot stay here at my landing point nor can I use my abilities to travel without being intercepted immediately. You must help me get to my destination. We have little time to spare, Sean." Her saying my name was enough to snap me back to the moment at hand. She must have seen my name on my name tag pinned on my sun visor.

"My only destination tonight is my apartment, space chick, and unless you plan on putting some money down on the pizza, you're not invited. So get the hell out of my van and carry on with whatever it is you alien chicks do." She looks forward as if thinking of what to say before connecting her eyes back to mine.

"I do not eat; therefore, I do not have to pay for anything."

Fuck. Not only does she have some knowledge of human ways, but she knows how to avoid the check.

"All I need is a normal escape away from a celestial situation that could cause both of us harm if we do not vacate the area fairly soon. This I can assure you." Her face has not shown much emotion since I met her, but now she looks worried, concerned even. Wait a fucking minute.

"What do you mean both of us?" I ask, taking my hands off the wheel while thinking of a way to get her out of my car somehow.

"We cannot stay here and discuss this any longer, Sean. We must leave here. I will do my best to hide my trail as we travel to buy us more time and not to alert any other people of my presence here."

Her breathing slows down as she inhales deeply and exhales loudly. The moon-like light emitting around her dims down to nothing, and her eyes close. At that moment, I could see her as a normal person. I realize that the pizza would most likely be cold if I don't leave here now, and one thing anyone knows about me is that my hunger can conquer all. I put the van in gear and drive off.

# 3.

We made it home to my apartment without any issues. The space lady was quiet the whole way here, but I'm not sure if she was sleeping or not. As soon as I killed the engine, her eyes opened. I manage to stop the pizza guy from leaving after promising him a big tip for making him wait. I would have just stopped for food on my way home, but I wasn't ready to go out and about with a half-naked girl from outer space just yet. On the drive home in silence, my mind was racing, trying to figure out if this is really happening. Also, my phone signal is dead since I encountered her. More importantly, where is she from and why is she here with me?

I stare at her with my mouth full of room temperature pizza while sitting at the small round table, cluttered with unopened mail and newspapers as she walks around my apartment as if she's investigating a fucking crime scene. Can't blame her though. My place isn't the cleanest and boxes were still piled up around the thrift shop furniture I brought to make the place more comfortable for my way of living. I had no plans to unpack because I'm planning to move back into the house my wife and daughter reside in. She stops and touches my punching bag propped up against the wall. She turns to me and smiles. "Are you some kind of fighter, Sean?"

I sigh and shake my head. "Something like that. I made my living by fighting, but it wasn't in any ring."

"This is incredible. This one fact alone ties our fates together. You may not be able to see it now, but when this is all over, you will understand," she says with excitement.

"When this is all over? This is over. I got you this far, but you'll have to go on foot or fly or whatever the hell it is you do. I'm in enough shit already trying to get my family back in order. I don't need you

9

adding to it."

"Sorry, Sean, this is already meant to be, and whether you like it or not, you're a part of this now," she says as she starts to walk closer to me.

"Let me get this straight, alien woman…"

"My name is not alien woman or space chick. I used to have a name, but it's one I can't remember now. It's hard to recall the memories from before I traveled here. You can help me make a new name. We can mark this as the start of you finally taking control of your fate. Try for something a little more fitting, please?" she says as she picks up a picture of a much younger me from the living room TV stand.

Her resolve is strong; strong enough to ignore everything I just said to her about my part in this fate thing, but my curiosity starts to set in, and now I want answers. "We'll circle back around to the name thing, alien. For now, I need some answers. Where the hell are you from and what are you doing here?"

She places the picture down where she got it from and wipes her hand on her poncho before moving along. "I did come from space but not originally; however, it's irrelevant to anything you need to know. I am here because I have to save a life." She continues to survey her surroundings, walking away from me and back over to the piled-up boxes as I eat my pizza, trying to wrap this whole evening around my head.

"Save a life? Whose life are you saving?"

"That information does not concern you at this moment, Sean," she says as she bends down to examine the older boxing bag that I didn't hang up. This punching bag was my first gift from a mob boss and it's tattered from all the beatings I gave it, showing from the duct tape wrapped all around it. Another relic of my past I should've thrown away with the rest of that life.

"I have been thrown slightly off course and need to get to the Evergreen Hospital in the city of Durham, North Carolina, to complete my task. And fate has it that you are the one to take me there. The one to be my guide and guardian.

"Guide and guardian," I respond in outrage, "I have to see my family tomorrow, and the best I can do for you is point you in the right direction. I don't know what I was thinking even bringing you this far...Kelly." She frowns immediately at the name to show her disgust. "Lisa?"

"No."

"Anabelle?"

"No."

"Summer?"

"No"

"Daisy?"

"No."

"What the fuck?"

"No."

"Eve, damn it!" I yell at her finally. "I'm calling you Eve whether you like it or not." For the first time, I see her smile and clap her hands together. I'm not sure whether to be scared or relieved.

"That's the spirit, Sean. You are my guardian now, and you have to be confident in the choices you make for me," Eve says as she comes over to me and what remains of the pizza.

"Let me stop you right there, Eve. What's the incentive to giving you what you want and for me to disregard my entire life for the next two to the three days to get you to NC? What do I get out of this deal other than time wasted?"

"I thought the self-satisfaction of saving the life of a fellow human being would be sufficient," Eve states as if to sway me. I raise an eyebrow at her and close the lid of the pizza box.

"Obviously you don't know who you're dealing with here," I respond in confidence.

Eve sighs and peers into my soul. Her prism eyes lock back on to mine as she speaks, "The other perk of being my guardian is that you must become cosmic. I will grant you the ability to open your being and connect to the universe, granting you power that has not yet been realized by humans for many centuries." She lifts her index finger and touches my forehead. I see the pupils of her eyes vanish, and a third eye appears in the center of her forehead; the same eye I saw her using when I found her in the woods. I can hear no sounds or feel anything at all, and I realize I'm no longer in my apartment. Somehow, I'm floating in outer space, gazing upon the stars and feeling the calmness of the galaxy. I've been high on drugs before but never experienced anything quite like this in my life. I could feel my heartbeat and the sensation of blood flowing through my veins.

"I am awakening your true potential, Sean." Eve's voice echoes as I float aimlessly through this space. "You need much more work than I anticipated, but at least, now I have opened the channel. I know the feeling may be intoxicating, but you will need to focus, Sean. Do you see any light present? One that resembles the sun or the moon?"

I could hear her questions clearly, but I couldn't respond yet. The feelings I felt through every nerve in my body were just overpowering any other functions.

"You cannot yet control the feeling, but we'll get there — one step at a time. For now, I'll just help your third eye free itself. With this, we'll be able to communicate freely in your space.

A jolt of energy bolted through my body. I could see a burst of colors of light cascading through the blackness of space. Moments I never thought about flash through my memory, so clear as if I'm reliving all of them at the same time. I could see strains of DNA, molecules, and atoms all swirling around one another. The sounds of glass shattering, bones cracking, gunfire, and children laughter echoed throughout my being. My body torpedoes through our solar system, passing planets I learned about in grade school before reaching Earth finally and slamming back into myself, sitting in a chair in my apartment. I fall out of my chair, catching myself with one hand and wiping the drool from my mouth with the other. The feeling is unexplainable. It's even better than sex. Everything around me is different down to the air I'm breathing. I hear myself panting, and I slow my breathing down. My head slowly rises, and I see Eve. She smiles at me as if she knows what's going to happen next. Collecting myself, I get back up to my feet as fast as I can.

"I'll get packed now. If we leave tonight, we can be there in less than two days or so." My mind was made up. That feeling was unlike anything I've ever felt. I'm already addicted to it, and I want more of it. I could hear my phone vibrating against the tabletop as it slid towards the edge. The sound of it brought me back to reality. My phone is getting a signal, again. I shake my head and slap myself on the cheek with my backhand as I answer it, expecting to hear my wife's anger sweltering through the speaker.

"Long time, no see, Sean, or should I call you Hammer?" A familiar male voice says with a slight Russian accent. "I never forgot what you and your boss did to my brother. I already took care of your old employer, and now it's your turn to pay the piper." There's a boom at the entrance door to my apartment. The sound of someone kicking in a door is a sound I'm all too familiar with. "That's your ride now. Don't keep me waiting, Hammer."

"Go to hell, Viktor," I reply and slam the phone against the table. I look over to Eve who's in the kitchen, pouring my two bottles of whiskey into the sink with a disapproving look on her face. She hasn't paid the not so friendly knock at my door any attention. "This stuff hampers your ability to connect, Sean. No wonder we have so much work to do." I give her elevator eyes, but before I could say anything, the door crashes open violently. Three guys rush into my apartment, wearing all black and holding batons. Clearly, Viktor wants to see me face to face to settle the score.

"Come quietly with us, and we won't hurt you or your girl in the kitchen there," the one in the back says with his ski mask muffling his voice. "Otherwise, you both got problems."

Three guys, Viktor? Surely, he remembers my reputation, and I remember his family's – known for ruining the lives of others after a good beating if the victim survives. These three flunkies here are probably ready to carry that reputation.

"Did Viktor not tell you punks who you were dealing with?" I walk over from the table towards the first one at the door as he yells, "Wrong move, old fella." He was about to swing the baton at me, but two quick punches to his nose and eye drop him. The other two rush in over his body: one on my left and the other standing right in front of me. I eye both of them, waiting to see which one has the balls to attack me first. The one on my left swings the baton towards my head. I quickly duck out of the way and return upright with an uppercut to

13

his chin.

The thing I learned about fighting a long time ago when my old man used to rough me up is that everyone has a button. A button you hit, and it shuts them down. The uppercut to the chin wasn't his, but I know where the next striking points will have to be to find it.

The one in front of me swings at me while his friend stumbles backward, feeling the uppercut. I dodge the strike by throwing my right shoulder back while bringing my left fist up to jab his eye. His head snaps back, leaving his chest open for my boot. He trips over his unconscious friend. The uppercut victim was back in the fray now, but he had abandoned the baton. He tackles me, throwing us both to the floor and pushing the table to the wall. He lands a punch to my right jaw. My anger from the pain gives me the extra strength to grab his collar and headbutt him. Blood pours from his nose as I roll him off me. Just as I get to my knees and ready to deliver another blow, one of the others recovers and rushes me with a yell. I cover my head with my elbows and forearms as he bashes the baton on them without control. I yell as the pain vibrates through my arms with every blow. I have to stop him before he does any more damage. I uncover myself just as he hit me the last time, and I scoop him from under his groan, spin into the air and drop him flat on the table which collapsed under the pressure of the fall. I climb on top of him and deliver two blows to his face. All three guys are down now, but one is still conscious. "I'll teach you mother fuckers a lesson tonight." I stand up and rub the pain along my forearms. I set my sight on a baton and pick it up.

"We must leave here!" Eve yells with fear in her voice. I imagine the scuffle here might have shaken her up. I glance over at her, standing there with my backpack I just packed, cuffed between her arms and her chest. "He'll know I've been here since I opened your channel, and we cannot let him find us. Not yet. We are not ready."

I look at the guy on the floor who's trying to stop the blood pouring from his nose and look back at Eve. "I'm not worried about any goon that comes after me, Eve," I say in full cockiness, "Tell Viktor I send my regards, and this better be the end of this, or he'll be..." I was interrupted by the patter of Eve's footsteps as she rushes out of the apartment. I look through the mess and pick up my cell phone.

"What's got her so spooked?"

I run after her.

# 4.

"This is nothing like a normal asteroid crash site, doctor. The angles are all wrong here, and the geometry just doesn't add up. If it came from above, directly above and landed here, how could it have made these skid marks afterward?" I state as he kneels, surveying the area where the crash occurred, his lab coat tail resting on his khaki pants so as not to get it dirty. We were in such a rush to get here; he didn't bother to take it off. "There is little to no traces of anything occurring after the crash. Even if the debris would have burned into ash or evaporated somehow, this means it was hot enough to burn the leaves and branches of those trees, yet they're untouched. What do you make of all this, Dr. Carson?" I ask.

"I've been researching stars, meteors, and all things outside of our atmosphere for many years, Samuel, and I have yet to come across anything like this before. Normally, these crash sites are out of our reach to get to, never landing this close to our offices. We don't have many options here, and unfortunately, we lack the light and crew to study the site properly which was the sacrifice of coming here so quickly. We'll have to return here during the daylight hours to see if we can make sense of any of this with the power of natural light," Dr. Carson says as he looks down at his flashlight and makes his way over to his toolbox. He opens it and throws me a roll of yellow caution tape to mark off the area. I catch the tape but drop the flashlight in the process. It's easier to cordon the site with both hands. I walk over to the nearest tree to start the tape when a boot steps out from the tree line, the boot cascading the end of my light's beam. The man appears to be triple my size without question and double the size of Dr. Carson. The stranger's silhouette startles me, making me fall backward. Now that the light is in my reach, I snatch it, shining it at the face of the stranger. Then I see his eyes squint over a neatly trimmed beard and mustache.

"My apologies, sir. This area is now closed to the public. We are in the process of sectoring it off for the next twenty-four hours by orders of the…aaaahhh." I drop the light to the ground, taking a small gasp of air as the intruder picks me up by my neck with one hand. The doctor hears my muffled distress and shines a light over to see me suspended in the air by this Neanderthal, my feet dangling as if there was no ground below them at all. Dr. Carson examines the freakishly large man as life is being strangled out of my body.

"Are you the thing that fell from the sky?" Carson asks him as he makes his way over to us. He steps softly around the crash site to get a closer look at the thing choking me in mid-air with one hand, showing overpowering strength. "We aren't here to hurt you. We are mere scientists just researching what happened here." The doctor eases his free hand behind his back, gripping his tranquilizer gun, no doubt.

The beast finally releases his grip, dropping me to the ground. I land on my backside, holding my throat, finally able to get a full breath of air again. I have no time to wallop in my pain now. This must go on record for the sake of science.

"No, you fool," the giant replies angrily. My name is Felix, and I am born and raised by Gaia herself. Taken from her womb and grown into adulthood to protect her for the eons to come, but that is beyond your concern. What are you two doing here? How do I know you are who you say you are and not the ones that crashed here tonight?" He takes his first few steps towards Dr. Carson. Somehow, I could only see this ending in aggression.

"Now I may be a strange-looking man in my old age, but I can assure you that we both are here in the name of science, earth science to be exact. Now stop right where you are, or I will be forced to make you.

Felix curls his lips up into a smile as he continues his approach. "I'd like to see you try, doctor."

Dr. Carson obliges and draws his gun, firing a tranquilizer right into the neck of the stranger. Carson knows it would take more than one shot to bring down a man of his size, so he instantly starts to load up another round, dropping his flashlight for quicker reloading, the jolt causing the light to turn off. With Felix still moving forward, I saw the dart hit his neck. These darts are made to stick into the skin of its

17

target, yet I could've sworn it just bounced right off him. I'm certain the doctor saw it, but he doesn't have time to second guess. He finishes loading up another shot and aims it at his aggressor, but this time, the large man stops about two steps away from him. Dr. Carson watches him with the weapon trained on him. His eyes seem to glow a greenish hue, and his head turns, looking off into the distance, eyes still gleaming. I'm not sure if this is some weird way of light refracting from our lights or if his eyes are indeed glowing.

"I've been wasting all my time here with you two for nothing. The star has already started using its aura and not very far off from here. I'll have to act fast to catch her. Looks like you are who you say you are after all. Carry on with your science," Felix says as he walks off into the tree line. Dr. Carson places his gun back in his waistline and grabs the flashlight only to see it has been crushed as if a boulder landed on it. He knows the guy was abnormally big, but no man could crush these titanium flashlights with bodyweight alone. They were made for space usage after all and built to withstand large amounts of pressure.

"Dr. Carson," my voice struggles to call to him. It startles him as he looks in the direction, he saw me last, but I'm no longer there. I managed to get to the camera and recorded the rest of the encounter that Dr. Carson had with Felix. "I've got it all here in night vision, doctor." Dr. Carson smiles as he sees the refraction of light that I'm aiming at him, flash from something on the ground. It was the first tranq he used against Felix. The smile swiftly left his face as he sees that the sharp end of the dart is bent upon itself.

# 5.

I watch the door chimes in the silence of the twenty-four-hour diner we arrived at about twenty minutes out of the city, away from the crash site. The door opens, and a man in a dirty uniform sits at the counter. Eve insisted we get out, far away from my apartment, but I wasn't sure why. I agree with her, seeing how three of Viktor's punks are licking their wounds on my dining room floor. She hasn't said anything the entire ride here either. Her silence is the least of my worries now that the mob is on my tail. The main reason we stopped here is that I called Herman and insisted, he meet us at the diner. I need information, and I need to know how much Viktor knows about me. Herman is the one that helped me disappear in the first place. I wonder where his loyalty lies as Eve stares through the window. I catch the twinkle in her eyes as she gazes out into the night street. I gave her a pair of the wife's red sweatpants and sandals out of my bag. The summer nights here can get humid, but most venues around here keep it cool inside, especially at night. I can't go out with her in public with just that poncho she's wearing. Although Eve's hips aren't quite as wide as Jasmine's. It's nothing a tight pull of the drawstring couldn't fix. She keeps the poncho on. Not much of a match, but it will have to do for now.

"My friend will be here soon and then, we can get a hotel so we can get some rest," I say to Eve to try and crack the ice with her all over again. "I mean, you do sleep, don't you?" She doesn't take her eyes from the window, but I see her gaze go upward. "I know you mentioned not needing food, earlier? Do you have to sleep at least?"

"Sleep is not something I need to function, but to sustain this form and hide my aura, I must. The same thing for eating; because this form needs it for sustainment. If I stay in my natural state, the one you found me in, I need none of these things. However, the more human I am while we are traveling, the less likelihood of us running into serious problems. We should already be on our way there to save this person's life, guardian. What are we waiting for exactly?" she says, turning her eyes to me.

"We're waiting for my friend to show up here and for him to tell me how much Viktor knows about my life. I can't just leave my family here helpless while I run off with some broad on some strange quest. Not just that, but I have to see my daughter, Jada, tomorrow morning before we can go anywhere," I say as I pull the phone from my pocket and place it on the table. I hit the button to see her adorable little six-year-old face, smiling back at me as Jazzy holds her. They look so much alike, and it's crazy. I notice my phone battery is getting low, so I go into my pocket. The waiter from behind the counter waves a hand towel at us to get my attention. I look up at him as I place my solar USB power bank charger on the table and plug it up. God knows I love my gadgets. "I'll take some coffee and a pancake stack for the lady over here." He nods and vanishes into the kitchen.

"I saw a photo of your family as I was looking around your dwelling, and they are lovely. I would hate for anything to happen to them. However, you will not be able to see, help, or save them if Gaia's guardian catches us. I do not stand a chance against him in combat, and you have not awakened your celestial connection. No matter how tough or strong you are to others here, you will have no effect against him until you do." She stops to shake her head from side to side to reiterate her message and continues, "Therefore, all we can do for now is move unnoticed and hope to get to the dwindling life before he catches us."

I rub my forearms under my long sleeve shirt to soothe the beating they took with the baton earlier. "I've taken on some pretty nasty odds, Eve. I think I can handle this guy. Can't we just finish connecting me or whatever so it would be one less thing we have to worry about?"

"The process cannot happen in one session, especially with someone so dislodged from the universe as you are," she replied, curving one side of her lips as she continues, "The other downside to that is I would have to use my ability to usher your connection, and that is how we will be found and destroyed. I will continue to train you as I have promised, as long as we make it to the hospital. If I help you connect now, you would have no reason to escort me. I'm not sure if you are a man of your word, Sean."

I sigh as another waitress brings us our orders. A thin, fair-skinned woman with a name tagged that says "Missy". Probably a nickname, but I wouldn't be surprised if it wasn't given the area. She pours my coffee and hurries over to the man at the counter.

"I'm gonna need a drink to swallow this shit." Her brow frowns, and her hands slam on the table with a slight impact, shaking it.

"This is why you are so far away from your connection. You can no longer drink any alcohol. It is a center altering substance, and with it, you will never be able to connect. You must also watch your language. It's not a good example to set for someone on such an ordained journey. It's all for the sake of finding your way, Sean," she whispers as she grabs my hands. Her initial touch is cold but then warm instantly. "Being celestial goes beyond physical force; you must also know discipline and patience. It will take all that you are, but I am confident that you have what it takes. It is fate, after all, Sean."

"Am I interrupting something here?" asks a voice next to the table. I look to see a thin man in an olive-green jacket with all kinds of superhero and video game patches sewed on it. His dyed red hair goes down to his shoulders, and his bangs touch the top of an eccentric glasses frame. I haven't seen him in quite a while, but I knew at first glance who it could be. "Things must be getting rough between you and the ole ball and chain, huh? I really liked her, Sean. Very pretty woman." Herman stops speaking as he looks at Eve and then back at me without skipping a beat. "She's pretty too, but she doesn't look like your type. Looks too young and too thin. Looks like she-"

"Herman!" I yell louder than I should've and startle the rest of the diner audience. I look around, embarrassed, so I take it down to my normal pitch. "Why the heck does Viktor know where I am? Why did I have to fight off three of his goons tonight if you gave me a clean identity and nothing traceable back to my old life?" Eve slides over as Herman takes a seat next to her along the bench. She slides her pancakes down to her end and starts to examine them, tilting her head sideways as she pokes at it with her finger.

"Viktor managed to find you, Sean? Guess the days of being the muscle is catching up to you. My programs and products are made to hide people in plain sight, yes. As I said when I offered you this, it's no sure shot, especially if you don't go across the nation. If someone really wants to find you and they have the resources and people to do it, then they will. You have to have known that messing with one of the most powerful men in the underworld would land you in his crosshairs eventually, whether it be one of his men looking for you or his very own surviving little brother, Viktor, in your case. He's probably taking Vinny's spot as…"

"I get it, Herman. I couldn't go far without my family. Jasmine agreed to move out of the city, but she didn't want to live far from her hometown, and that's why I couldn't go further. Viktor called me and said he already got to Sebastian as if he already wasted him." Herman looks over at Eve as she starts to eat the pancakes without syrup or utensils. He didn't think too much of it considering he is far from normal himself.

"Well, maybe that's how he found you. He found him first, tortured him into giving up some info about you, then murdered him for killing his older brother, and now he wants to do the same to you. Man, the life of a thug is really doggy dog. What goes around comes around. You should have taken up another profession. You could've used your powers for good and been a WWE wrestler."

I wave my hand in front of his face to interject. I've known this motor mouth for years. The only way to get a word in when he starts up is to just blurt it out while he speaks. "Listen, Herman. I'm not concerned about Viktor and what he wants. I'll deal with him and whatever he has coming my way. I need to know if he can connect me back to my family at all. He slouched down into the seat and looked straight up at the ceiling for a moment before looking back down at me. "I changed everything I could find connecting you to Jasmine in any way. Finding you is hard enough but finding anything else would be hella hard. Like scaling the side of a building covered in a sheet of ice naked and barehanded-hard. Like super hard. You get my point. Speaking of which, who's she?"

"This is the other thing I mentioned on the phone we have to speak about. This is my new friend, Eve. Eve, meet Herman. I just met her earlier tonight off Route Seventeen on my way home from work. She's out of this world, literally." I look at her as she is scarfing down what's left of the pancake she's holding. "She's an alien or a Martian of some kind." Herman's eyes widen as he tilts his head down and looks over the top of the frame of his glasses, giving Eve a once over. With him being the sci-fi freak that he is, I don't see him having a hard time believing me.

"She looks like an ordinary babe to me, Hammer. I'm going to A: need proof or B: know what drugs you've consumed in the last twenty-four hours." Eve finishes the pancake and turns her attention to Herman. I take a sip of the black coffee, instantly frowning from bitterness. "Well, you heard the man, Eve. Proof."

"I'm not of this world, Herman, just as Sean has stated. I am an anomaly in time and space, the product of knowledge and knowing one's self, connected to this realm and giving life by a star. This is the moment in time I was fated to be a part of, and now I am here with you all. Sean has agreed to take me to the Evergreen Hospital in North Carolina where a life that needs saving hangs in the balance. While enroot, I will attempt to teach him to use his celestial connection. I'm not the first of my kind to land here, and I will not be the last, but learning what I know now about my creation and this planet, I am the first one here in over thirty years," she says as she stares relentlessly into Herman's eyes. By now he's noticed the fraction of color dancing around her pupils and the eerie feeling she radiates.

"You may have the unique eye colors to back up your claims, but I still need physical proof you are something other than human," he nonchalantly responds as he points over to my phone on the solar panel charger. "Is that the same phone Viktor called you on, Hammer? He's probably got some tech head like me, tracking your every movement by now."

I'm sure he was right about that, but I'm also counting on it. "He can track me all he wants. If I can keep him away from my family, there is nothing to be concerned about, and stop calling me Hammer. That's an identity and life I got away from, and I want to keep it that way, Herm." Eve picks up the cell phone and solar battery at the same time. The blinking indicators on the battery that pulses when the solar light is hitting it grows brighter than I have ever seen before. You can hear the phone begin to sizzle just before a light popping sound is heard. The smell of burnt electronics seeps through the edges. Herman stares at the phone and then back at Eve. Finally, he looks at me. "Looks like star power to me. Guess we better get some rest back at my place, seeing how yours is compromised. I have to grab a few things before we hit the road. There is no way I'm going to miss out on any of this crazy shit."

# 6.

We pull up into the quaint, quiet suburban neighborhood at 10:12 on this odd Friday morning. The yards of each of the two-story homes are neatly trimmed, and the grass is cut to mimic the greenery of golf courses. I'm sure the owners of these homes will get their lawns treated before Fall officially starts. Families were already out in the yard, playing with their young children or tending to their gardens. One man is even under the hood of an early '80s Camaro accompanied by his preteen son, possibly showing him the what's what of the mechanical beast. Families are meant to be together. They aren't designed to be apart like I am from mine. Jasmine and her deadbeat sister picked a great area to live after she left me. I gave her and our daughter the world, and she leaves me alone in the aftermath of my choices – choices I made for her and Jada to live like I was never able to. Herman pulls up to the curb and parks his Nissan Rogue. We ditched my van at the diner and stayed with Herm at his place overnight where we showered and rested up. Not sure how long he slept after quizzing Eve majority of the night. He's always been a talker, and I think he's naturally an insomniac. I think he's the type of guy who is always so involved in their own minds, that sleep evades them. Even though he rambles constantly, he knows how to stay off the radar using technology. That's one of his many services. I give him a nod before I step out of the car and make my way to the door. I do a quick straightening off my jeans and adjustment of my t-shirt before ringing the doorbell. My forearms still feeling the muscle soreness from the attack last night, but pain has never been a stranger to me. If anything, I consider pain as a close relative of mine, and it's always there for me, especially when I'm drunk and alone. The door clicks and swings open. Jessica, the dreaded sister-in-law, standing there with the scowl of resembling their mother, but her face is round and she weights slightly more than Jasmine. She never married. No children. Just plenty of attitude towards me.

"Well, looky what we have here," she says in a whimsy tone, "I'm surprised you were able to make it out here without catching a DUI or disturbing the peace."

"Yeah, but I'll catch a case for domestic violence if you don't get the fuck out of my face," I respond. "You know whose money you're using to live in this house, right? You should show me a little respect, woman. Anyway, I'm not here to argue with you right now. Where are my wife and daughter?"

"You ain't no saint, Hammer. I mean, how many people did you beat, hurt, or kill for this money? Don't even answer that. My sister is putting clothes on my niece," she snarls. "You know, you come over here, acting all big and bad, thinking that she wants you back, but she doesn't, clown. She'll never want a two-timing sidekick of some gangster to be around Jada. You can make it easier on everybody and stop coming around here because she's moving on. I'm sure you don't need any trouble with the law around here. I wouldn't involve them out of love for my sister, but one of these white people around here might think you're a suspicious-looking negro."

The anger slowly creeps outward onto my face as a frown slowly takes over, the more she speaks. Her mouth keeps moving, but I don't hear anything other than the annoying squawk of her voice. There were no more words that needed to be said to this poor excuse of a woman that's been living off my success for years. Eating our food and taking our money, parading around as if she isn't a nuisance. She's got under my skin for the last time. "I've had it up to here with you, you little…"

"Daddy!" Jada screams as she rushes towards the door. She comes out and jumps into my arms. I lift her and twirl her around as I take her a few steps off the porch. In this instant, I forget about everything. I only see her smile and hear her laughter. Just this moment alone makes the weight of reality go away.

"Hey, Jada, my little angel. How have you been, pretty girl?" I ask her. She smiles and hugs my neck. "I'm okay. I just miss you so much." Her adorable voice gives my soul happiness. "Daddy misses you too, baby. Don't worry, honey. One day, daddy will be able to see you every day like it used to be. We'll be together again. Her little face frowns, and she fiddles with her hands as she says, "Auntie said that I'm going to get a new dad, but I told her I don't need a new dad."

Fucking skank. I take Jada's chin and lift it to my face so I can stare into her cute little hazel eyes; a trait passed on down from her mother.

"I'll always be your dad, and I'll be with you forever and ever and ever." I toss her up in the air and twirl her around again. She smiles and giggles uncontrollably. As we spin, I catch a silver Mercedes pulling up into the driveway as Jasmine steps outside with her sister. I disregard the car when I see Jasmine standing there in all her ebony beauty. Staring at her pictures in my apartment can never come close to looking at the real thing. I put Jada down and take her hand as we walk towards the porch. "Good morning, Jazzy. You looking as fine as ever," I say as my heart flutters to see her in those tight jeans and v neck top, exposing some cleavage. Her makeup freshly done and her long straight black hair, that naturally shines, in a ponytail that stops right above the middle of her back. I could smell her perfume from here, sending a volley of memories through my head of all our steamy nights together. She scoffs and looks at me as if her eyes could shoot lasers.

"Yeah, whatever you say. Do you think I forgot about that fight you started with me last night before you hung up in my face and turned your phone off? You didn't even call me back," Jasmine's sharply states.

I knew I was going to get in trouble for that, but I think an alien encounter would make for a shitty excuse. "I didn't hang up on you, baby. My phone died, and I just ended up getting tied up last night, and I didn't get a chance to get back with you."

She simply shakes her head and releases a sigh. "You don't have to make excuses for me anymore, Sean. Where are you going to take your daughter today?"

"That's the thing, Jazzy. Something came up, and I have to take care of this before it gets out of hand." I couldn't tell her the truth. Not even the part about Viktor finding me and wanting me dead. She had enough of the death threats back when his big brother, Vinny, was after me before he died. I couldn't tell her that she could be right back in the same boat; a boat that I would put her in. A look of disappointment comes across her face, both Jazzy and Jada. Then suddenly, Jada runs away from us to some strange man in a button-up and slacks. His shirt is pressed neatly, and his shoes look expensive. She clutches his leg and turns her head away from me. "Jada, I'm sorry," I say as I look at the unknown man in the eyes from the porch as he lifts Jada into his arms. "Who's this, Jasmine?" I ask without looking back at her.

"His name is Kevin, and he's just a…"

"Put my daughter down now, Kevin," I firmly say to him as I take a few steps away from the porch. Don't you think it's rude to pick up another man's child without knowing the father?"

He pats her back softly before placing her down by his feet. "I never heard of this rule, Sean. Besides, I think we both know you don't get ahead of the game by playing by the rules," he says tauntingly as he looks past me and smiles at Jasmine. "You look amazing, Jasmine."

The next thing I know, I have my hands around his throat as he lays across the hood of his car with blood running down his nose. My knuckles are bruised, and his shirt is torn. Herman is there pulling me away from him. "You're killing the man, Hammer," he says fearfully in hopes of that breaking my trance and getting me off him. I release Kevin and take a few steps away from him but not because of Herman. I could finally hear my daughter crying and her mother yelling at me. Jasmine shoves me further away from the yard with tears welling up in her eyes.

"This is why we'll never be a family again. You've been a monster for so long, and you don't know how to be anything else. You're not a normal person, a husband, or a father. I love you, but I can't anymore," she says as her voice begins to whimper. She picks up Jada, as Jessica tends to Kevin. She glances at Herman and back at his silver SUV. I follow her stare and find Eve standing outside the car, looking with a straight face and her hands cuffing her elbows. I turn back to my angry wife as the tears drop from her eyes. "You got Herman and some random bitch with you, I see. Looks like you are going back to your old ways, Hammer. Just leave, and I don't care to see you ever again after today."

And just like that, my anger gives way to sadness. She ripped my heart from my beating chest as she turns away with Jada in her arms. My daughter didn't even do so much as look at me as I start to walk away. I've had some terrible moments in life, but knowing that Jasmine looks at me and could only see a monster… We all get back in the car. I can feel Herman's stare before he starts the car.

"Are you okay, Sean?" he questions. I nod and signal him to pull forward with a hand gesture. I might cry if I say anything and we have to get on the road. I'm sure Jessica wasn't too far from the truth about someone calling the cops on me, especially after my episode with Kevin. The last thing I need right now is for the law to be after this identity too.

# 7.

After stopping at a store and getting Eve some clothes for the next few days, we start our drive to the Evergreen Hospital. Herman decided to keep driving as I sit here contemplating my recent dose of bad choices. She called me a monster, and could I blame her? Jasmine and I have been together since our high school years, so she saw all the parts of me that no one else did. She's seen me fight groups of men or beat a man to an inch of his life all because Sebastian, my old employer, said so. I've always been a fighter. It goes back to a young me brawling with my dad as I grew up. He would slap my mom and me around. He's in jail for life now, but no telling what would've happened between us if the cops didn't take him. I blame him for my anger edge. I snap out of my train of thought and back to reality by the tapping on my shoulder from the backseat.

"She called you a monster, but you are much deeper than she can ever know, Sean," she says with hope in her prismed eyes. "I have felt your true potential, and I know there is more to you than this hard exterior."

I snort as I turn away from her. "I know you're trying to cheer me up, Eve, but there are parts of me and my past that you don't know about. A past full of a mixture of blood, scars, and broken bones."

"That's right, Eve," Herman follows up without missing a beat. "Our friend here real name is Marc Watkins, AKA Hammer. After working as the right-hand man and muscle for a very successful crime lord, he chose to disconnect himself from that life when his daughter Jada was born, and that's where I come in. I set him up with a new identity as Sean Carver, the cable guy.

Here he goes again. His mouth never fucking closes.

"Jasmine had enough though. Fed up with his lifestyle, she took

30

Jada and left him. Sean desperately holds on to his family with the money he earned for being Hammer. If only he could somehow get his family back, Eve, but after that little scuffle he did back there, I don't see it as a possibility. You better hope that man you were choking back there doesn't have friends in high places. With a car like that and those custom leather shoes, I think you may have messed with the wrong…"

"That's enough, Herman," I growl through clenched teeth. "Any other time and I would have stopped you from running your mouth about me, but I got a lot on my mind right now. Thanks for giving her my life story. You forgot to mention where I was born and raised though."

Herman shrugs it off "That sounds like sarcasm in your tone. I'm just saying, Hammer. You have a long history of breeding trouble no matter where or what you do. We've known each other for a long time, and I can't remember a time up until the identity change that you weren't fighting for something. Maybe you're just cursed with this 'born to fight your whole life' thing. You had to fight every other person in the streets and at home.

"Shut up now, Herman, or you'll be the next thing on my list to fight, and I don't think you can take a punch." My fist extends swiftly and stops inches away from his cheek. He flinches, grips the steering wheel tighter, and smiles nervously. "You're putting me in a really bad mood right now, and I should throw you a jab or two for calling me Hammer after I already told you that's a no go."

He pushes his glasses up to his face and cracks his window to get some fresh air against the heat of his clammy skin. "Point taken, Sean Carver. You won't hear it from me ever again. Just a bad habit that is remarkably easy to fix." I lower my arm and smirk to myself.

"I've seen your universe, Sean, and I know more about you than anyone else does," Eve says calmly, even after being told about my violent ways. "You can still turn everything around by achieving the connection; the power of becoming cosmic. I see that it troubles you greatly to be apart from your family despite your mistakes against them, but you can make things better." She places both of her hands gently on my shoulders. Her fingers begin to slide up my neck, making my skin tingle and the hairs stand up on my arms. "Herman, you continue to drive no matter what you see." Her hands touch the side of my head, and I suddenly feel cold as I close my eyes – the kind of cold that you feel down to your bones.

I open them to find myself back in darkness, floating aimlessly just as I was last night when she touched my forehead. I could see my breath as I begin to pant with anxiety. The cold now does more than just chill my bones but starts to freeze me. I wrap my arms around myself to warm up while the chill brings on a light pain all over my body, then I hear a faint whisper.

"Concentrate. You must believe in your universe and the power within it, Sean." It was Eve's calming voice reaching out to me but from where? "This is your universe, and you must treat it as such. First, we will begin by forming light. What will you choose to light your way, my guardian?" I say the first thing to come to mind.

"Stars?"

"Do not question it. You must believe in it and will it to be, Sean. Focus and believe." I try to focus, but the frost is starting to bear down on me. I start to shake uncontrollably. "You can do this, Sean. Use the strength of will here just as you used your fist out there." Her words hit my very core, making my blood boil. My body starts to warm up as I put my hands together, focusing and willing what will happen next. I open them with my palms facing up and there lies a ball of light. I could see now. The darkness still stretched out all around me for as far as I could see, but the light in my palms could show me the way to my inner clarity. Looking next to me, I see Eve speaking over my shoulder to see the very light she helped me create. Was she there the whole time, guiding me through the darkness? I throw the light into the air and watch it illuminate the pitch-black.

"You can do this, Sean," she says as she smiles at my achievement. "If you keep stepping in this direction, I can promise you, you will have your family back if you will it to be, or maybe you will choose otherwise when the moment comes. I want you to understand that you are the master of your world, both in here and out there."

At this moment, my heart feels the vibration of Eve's words. It's as if anything is possible. As I will myself to stop floating, stand on my feet, and watch the light that came from my own two hands, it all begins to make sense. A star shining within this place of void and despair represents one thing. That one thing is something I lost sight of for many years but can see it now, more clearly than ever before: hope.

\*\*\*

My morning start was going great before I showed up here and got news of someone else quitting. Pulling another double shift at the diner is the last thing I wanted to do today until the sexiest man I've ever laid eyes on scrolled into the place. He looks like he's big enough to pick up cars and fling them like matchboxes. I've never seen him around here before, but I would love to know more about him. After observing him for a few minutes as he looks around the diner, I could see he's in search of someone. He's looking for you, Allie. He just doesn't know it yet.

"Hey, darling, I'm right over here," I shout at him while staring at his bulging muscles underneath his shirt. "I can take your order right over here, handsome." He glances up at me only for a moment as he walks over to a table and stares. He sighs as he takes a seat, still looking puzzled as if things were out of place. I'm sure a fresh cup of coffee will help jump-start his day, so I strut over there with the biggest smile, holding our freshest pot of coffee in our cleanest mug. "The menu is upright behind the napkin dispenser, dear. This cup of coffee is on me." I pour the coffee into the mug as his head swivels around to the menu and back up to me. Our eyes lock, and I take notice of a strange burst of green in the center of his hazel eyes. I've never seen anything like it. His lips move, but I don't hear anything that he says. His whole appearance is a distraction.

"Ma'am, I asked if you've been working throughout the night?" he repeats, his voice deep and clear. I simply shake my head without looking away from his eyes as my heart starts to race. He places a picture of a black man with a couple of scars on his face and what looks to be his wife and daughter smiling happily on the table. The scars were freshly healed but still had more healing to go. "Is there someone that was working here throughout the night that I can speak to? It's vital that I find this man."

"Yeah, we have Missy, who's been here all night, and she never forgets a face. She's in the back now probably getting ready to get out of here. Want me to get her for you, Mister…"

"Just call me Felix, and yes, I would like to speak with her for a moment."

I shout out for Missy as loud as I could. That usually works to get her attention because I'm not taking my eyes off this big hunk of a man. "She should be up here any moment," I say. Now, Missy is a young girl with a much thinner frame than myself, so I have to act fast if I want to let him know I'm interested before that hussy tries to move in on my prey. "Are you from around here, Felix?"

"Not exactly. I'm just passing through for work purposes."

"You must be a long way from your family out here. Your wife and kids must really be missing you."

"I'm not married, nor do I have any children."

"Oh. So, your girlfriend?"

"Don't' have one or time for one."

"Not the commitment type. Just out looking for a good time then?"

"Where the hell is Missy?"

"She'll be here any minute. You know, I'll be off work in another twelve hours. You should hang around so I can show you around town. We can hit all the hotspots," I whisper to him through my seductive smile.

Felix narrows his eyes at me and walks away from the table without giving me another look. He reaches the countertop and yells, "Missy!" His yell was deep, and it feels as if the whole place had rumbled to the bass of it. Missy burst through the kitchen doors and stop instantly after seeing who shouted out to her. I made my way over to him, disregarding the other patrons that were trying to get my attention to order, but I had my eyes and work efforts set on Felix.

"I'm Missy, sir, and how can I help you?" she said with a slight tremble in her voice. She was probably taken aback by his presence and a body that looked to be chiseled out of stone. Felix shows her the picture and asks her the same thing he asked me about the photo. She barely looks at the picture before responding, "Yeah, he was here with two other people sitting at that booth there." She points her polished nail to the table that Felix was just sitting at.

"Two others?" he questions and looks back at the photo before continuing. "Who did you see with him?"

"It was a weird dressed young girl with dark hair and pale skin, and later a redheaded man that wore glasses came in to meet them at the table. Is he in trouble? Are you in law enforcement?"

I follow up on the question, grabbing his forearm lightly and saying, "I bet you're the best in the business, huh, Felix?"

"Allie, get off that man!" Missy says aggressively. He looks at me before looking away, but not at anything in the diner. You would think he could see through the walls the way his head slowly turns. A satisfying smile spreads across his face as if he just realized something major. He peels me off his arm with his free hand and sits me in the stool next to him. "Thank you both for your assistance." He hurries out of the diner, making a beeline past the cars and trucks in the parking lot. I run out to see him leave and maybe get a chance to give him my number, but he runs and jumps into a small patch of trees and bushes opposite the diner. I wait to see if he reemerges through the other side, but he never does. It was like he jumped in and vanished.

"Stop chasing him and get back to work!" Missy shouts. "We'll never have any regular customers if you keep harassing all the good-looking men that come in here."

# 8.

"That was the craziest thing I've ever witnessed, Sean," Herman screams as he barely manages to keep the car on the road. "She clearly had a third eye that appeared when she touched you. I have to be honest and the weirdness of everything happening since last night and the little incident with your phone in the diner was borderline parlor tricks, but now that I've seen what she just did, I am a believer. Eve, you really are a unique lifeform from another reality or space or whatever. In fact, can we clarify which one of those you actually are? I mean I know I saw you use some kind of UV energy last night to blow up Sean's phone, but what kind of being can create its own UV energy source? You're like the most amazing girl I've ever known. Wait. Are you a girl at all or is this some type of intergalactic illusionary skin that you're using to sway us to believe that you come in-"

"Herman," I spout, rubbing my temples, not sure if it's from the training session Eve just put me through or his wild and splotchy commentary. "Cool it for just a few minutes, will ya? I need to take a quick breather, so be sure to pull over at the next gas station." I look over at his fuel gauge. "Looks like you could use some more gas, so we'll kill two birds with one stone." He nods and looks back at Eve through the center rearview mirror, probably waiting for a response from her.

"That should jump-start your centering process, Sean. I am only able to walk you through so much with us being tracked by the Gaius. So, I planted a part of myself into your psyche to help guide the rest of the process. Whenever you're ready to continue the training, you just need to remember the sensation you just felt when you created your own light. It is not as difficult as it may seem. It is like using a muscle that you have never used before," Eve explains. "The headache or nauseous feeling you may get is your body's reaction to acclimating itself with the universe. It may come and go throughout your training, but once completed, you may never feel the sensation again."

"So what happens when he completes the training, Eve? What exactly will he gain from all this?" Herman asks. For once, our thoughts were on the same wavelength.

"Several things will happen during the process. He will finally be able to

36

center himself and gain all kinds of attributes such as enhanced durability, strength, and speed beyond that of human conception. Completing the training will make you a cosmic being and becoming this opens doors to unimaginable powers. It varies from being to being, so I cannot predict what the universe will gift you with. It all lies in your fate," she answers in full certainty. Herman's head nods as he accepts the information. I could see the calculation in his mind starting to formulate some unorthodox universe where I'm some sort of god. With the way Eve made it sound, it wasn't too far from the truth.

"So you're saying he'll be some kind of superhuman person?" he questions with his eyes squinted at her in the rearview mirror. She shakes her head and looks over at me. "No such thing as a superhuman, Herman, but his connection to the universe will make him superior compared to the average human. For example, do you still feel any pain from your encounter with those men that barged into your dwelling last night, Sean?"

Now that she mentions it, I haven't felt it in the last couple of minutes. I take a look at my forearms and see that the bruising has almost vanished completely. I can't believe this is truly happening to me.

"This means your normal attributes have been jolted by the centering process. The more steps you complete, the more you restore your connection to the universe, and it will cause your body to act accordingly."

Herman turns into the gas station and pulls around next to a pump when he asks, "Why do you say restore his connection to the universe? Was he connected to the universe before?"

"Yes. All humans are born with a connection to the universe, but from what I can see, the older you become, the more your connection dwindles. I'm not sure of the cause of all this, and I'm sure it can be related to several things such as the food you eat to the stress you acquire with aging."

We all open our doors and get out of the vehicle. My mind is racing, and I'm not sure how I come to be a part of all this space stuff. I'm the last person who is worthy of these powers. I must admit, this all is too awesome to fathom. Herman's phone rings as I leave the bathroom and proceed to the gas pump outside while Eve was walking around and staring at everything oddly and trying on hats. I watch the pump as the numbers start to increase. The gas station is a small one. It's nothing like a truck stop, but it's a typical station you'll find outside any neighborhood. These pumps don't have the fancy TVs at the top of them with all the advertising and news castings. They weren't too old either. I only had to press the 87 button to start the pump. I start to take in the peacefulness of the environment when suddenly, a black SUV pulls up behind me, brakes squealing to a halt. Four men hop out of the car with speed, wearing tailored suits. The driver had a nose strip over his face beneath his sunglasses. He was one of the guys from last night. It must be Viktor's crew, but how did they find me all the way out here.

"You're coming with us, Hammer," says the man on the passenger side as I put the gas pump away and begin to twist the fuel cap back on. "We don't want to hurt you just yet. Make this easier on yourself," he says with determination in his eyes — the same determination in mine when Sebastian would send me out on a retrieval. I only saw one of their faces last night. I'm not sure if this was the same crew of guys plus one or not. It didn't matter at this point. Either way, I was outnumbered.

"I don't know if Viktor told you guys about me or not, but I'm not the type to go down without a fight folks," I say, making my way to them and cracking my knuckles. I look over at the driver – the one from last night – and flash a quick smile. "What's your name, kid?" He fixes his shades and smiles back at me. "I'm Ram. You got lucky with my boys and me last night, but your luck is up today."

I laugh at his invalid truth. "You think because you got another body with you that this will even up the odds against ole Hammer, eh? I don't know if your boss informed you, kid, but I don't think there has ever been a way to even the odds with me. In this world, either you are the nail or the hammer. In this scenario boys, I'm the hammer." Ram's thumb points at the guy over his shoulder, and he moves his suit coat slightly out of the way of his waistline, revealing a pistol. After taking notice of the first armed goon, I see the bulge of another guy's waistline. Probably not because he's happy to see me either. That's the new school way of making people do what you want around here now. People are scared to take a beating nowadays. I swallow nervously and nod my head. There is only one thing to do to deal with this situation, especially if you don't want the bitch seat. "I call shotgun."

The goons from the back seat snatch me up as Ram battered face grins. I'm not sure how they found me here, but I'm going to get to the bottom of this once I think of a way to stop my abduction. I've been in worse predicaments than this, and I've learned with a little patience and timing, there is always a way out. Ram stops the guy ushering me to the middle back seat of the SUV and punches me in the stomach. A groaning sound manages to heave its way out of my mouth as the back-seat twerp pushes me into the center seat. They all enter the car around me. My eyes catch a glimpse of Herman and Eve coming out of the store in disbelief. Eve's expression drastically changes when the SUV starts to peel out of the parking lot. I have to get my thoughts together if I plan to get out this alive. I close my eyes and decide that doing something rash and reckless was the only way out. Who am I kidding? Rash and reckless is what I've been known for all these years. The SUV was halfway out of the gas station parking lot when something smashes into it. I could feel the right side of the vehicle jolt into the air before landing on flattened tires and busted rims.

"What the fuck was that?" Ram yells, recovering from the shock of the accident. I shake away the haze just in time to see the rear passenger window burst open. Glass flies through the air, and I shield my eyes to protect them when I see the goon next to me being ripped out of the vehicle, through the shattered window. My mouth drops as I lay eyes on one of the biggest men I've come across. His arms are as big and round as watermelons. His face looks like it could have been chiseled from metal. The man skims the foot soldier once and drops him to the ground. The front passenger door opens, and the big guy's attention is already on him. The passenger rushes the guy, but I saw this as my window of opportunity. I don't care about the outcome. The driver door flings open, and Ram draws his pistol, aiming it at the tyrant that just mangled the other members of his crew. I start to climb over the back seat, making my way for the rear door exit. I get over the back of the seats feeling like a five-year-old in his mother's soccer van – a task not easy for a full-grown man.

I fall out of the hatch, landing on my back. I wince in pain, and I see the two bodies of the other men collide with Ram and the other passenger. But that couldn't be. Did he single-handedly throw both of those men at the same time and over the top of the SUV like that?

"What the hell is going on here?" I mumble as I jump to my feet but standing in front of me is the big guy who looks more intimidating when you see him face to face. His eyes fixate on me as he pulls a picture from his pocket, glimpses at it, and then flicks it to my feet.

"I finally found you, and I can't let you go any further." His deep voice seems to echo through my bones when he speaks. "If you tell me where the star is, I just may spare your life."

The guy looks like a mountain, but I never backed down from anyone no matter the size or position. "I don't know what you're talking about. Would you like to explain what kind of steroids you're taking because I've met some big guys in my day, but none like you." I say as I grab the picture he took out of the frame in my apartment and stuff it in my pocket. This is the guy tracking Eve. He must have felt her use her powers when she jumpstarted my connection in my apartment last night. Incredible. "What the hell are you?"

"I am Felix, and I know you have the star in your possession. I could feel her at your dwelling, and I felt her essence down the highway. If you don't want to tell me, then I'll have to force you to tell me." He takes a big step towards me right as a gunshot sounds out from behind me, leaving my ears ringing as I duck out and run away from the scene into the road. Another SUV with Herman at the wheel and Eve sitting shotgun pulls up right in front of me and squelches to a stop.

"Get in!" he shouts over the gunfire behind me.

"The star." Felix's mutters could be heard clearly over the gunfire. He is the calmest of us all.

I look back as I jump into the rear passenger seat and see the black SUV being pushed over on its side as we peel off down the highway, full speed ahead. Looking out the back window, I could see the mountain of a man staring down the street at us as we make our escape.

# 9.

"Their similarities are remarkable, Samuel," I whisper to my assistant as I study the photos in front of me. "I knew my theory would be looked at as insanity, but as I told you many times before, science is nothing but a thin line between reality and insanity. Great men, scientists rather, were all called crazy when they discovered their formula that would later make their mark in history." I take a push pin and hang the photo up on my corkboard next to all the other jumbled up photos and sketches of Felix. I grab more coffee to help keep my mind sharp. I've always lack sleep when I come across a find.

"I'm not exactly sure what you mean here, doctor. I see all the photos that you have up, but I just arrived. After what happened last night, I needed a good night's rest, so you're going to have to catch me up on what you got going on here this lovely afternoon. Judging by the fact you're still in the clothes you were in when we were out in the woods last night, you haven't showered yet." Samuel says through a cricket smile. He is indeed not the most attractive assistant, but he was the only one to believe in my studies back when I stepped down from the NASA Research Division.

"It's fine. I'll explain everything to you step by step. Now, you remember the big fellow we came across last night in the woods while looking for the star?" Samuel nods as he takes the pot of coffee and pours himself a cup in his own mug from home. He knows that I haven't been the cleanest man ever since I got a hold of this idea years ago. "Well, I wasn't sure because I couldn't get a good look at him until you left the footage with me last night. I thank you for helping me and for also using the night vision option on the camera. Because of you, I was able to come away with this still frame of him. I was able to compare this image to another image I remember seeing at another crash site in El Paso over twelve years ago." I point to the image of a large shadow walking through the desert towards the dust of the crash. Samuel squints his eyes and stirs his coffee quietly. "The camera is too far away as is the technology we were using back then, so I took a step further. I used my connections from the research team to get more recent footage of any meteors or space debris landing on our planet in the last four years or so, and they sent me some high definition footage of six incidents that meet my criteria."

"Let me interject here for a second, Dr. Carson. Did you stay up all night watching those videos? Any night footage taken from NASA camera feeds could last for hours and hours, days even." Samuel says, moving some paperwork out of the way to clear a seat to sit down.

"No, I wasn't able to watch all the videos, but saw enough to find something that caught my interest, which is what I'm about to tell you about now." I point at another picture on the board without turning to watch his reaction. "This image was captured two years and some odd months ago." The image shows our unsavory friend from last night appearing at another suspected crash site of some kind. I could see Sam giggling to himself before he starts to speak.

"I apologize, Dr. Carson. It's just that the image reminds me of a bad photograph of Big Foot." He places the coffee down and walks over to all the images to get a closer look. "So, if this is him, doctor, these images show that he's been at almost every crash site for a few years. It's like he's been looking for something to touch down here. Given his tone with us the last night and the fact that he was inhumanly strong and could withstand those darts, we can say he's someone that may or may not be of this world."

"That or he could be one souped-up muscle head with a god complex and a love for shooting stars," I state, doubting my research. After hearing myself explain it, the probability of our encounter being what my theory says is close to zero, but it's always that point zero one percent that can turn this all around." Sam finishes his coffee and places the mug down. He grabs his lab coat and the remote from my nightstand.

"I'm going to check out the rest of this footage myself and get to the bottom of this," he says with his hopes renewed. "You should probably get some rest. Samuel Richards is on the case, and I won't let you down, doctor." I always wanted to say that.

# 10.

Ten minutes have passed while I remain looking out the backseat window to see if that monster is following us. No one said a word. Herman is just getting his thoughts together, probably wishing he had some kind of anxiety medication to help him relax, while Eve is just gazing out of the window, unmoving. Then there is me who is just calming down from almost being kidnapped and killed. Not to mention the encounter with Felix, who looks to me is bullet resistant, but I couldn't tell. He asked about the star; about Eve. I'm not sure how Viktor's men had found us outside the city, but I need answers.

"Now that no one is trying to kill me, I need some answers from both of you, pronto. Let's start with what I'm used to encountering," I say, tapping Herman on the shoulder. "Would you like to explain to me why Viktor knew where we were?"

"Seems he's been tracking your phone and mine since you came under attack yesterday. He called me when I was walking into the gas station yesterday, just as his men pulled up to grab you. Don't worry though, I ditched the phone and got us two prepaid phones for now. I want you to know that I'm not working for Viktor in any way, shape, or form," Herman expresses. He doesn't lie to his friends or set people up. It's totally out of his character even if it has been a couple of years since we did business, and that was when he changed my identity and kept my family off the radar. I've seen him hold out under pressure before, and I know he would do the same for me. I still trust him.

"I believe you, and thanks for picking me up off the street back there before it got nasty with the big guy, Felix, which brings me to my next question." I look at Eve as she finally turns her head to look at me through the front rearview mirror. Sunlight appears to dance in her eyes, dazzling enough to hypnotize, so I focus my eyes on the back of her head instead. "Would you like to explain what in the hell happened back there?"

"It was the craziest shit I have ever seen, Sean," Herman interjects. "That guy you called Felix; shoulder charged the front of the car like he was a tank. He had everyone inside that gas station in awe before he snatched the guy out of the backseat with one hand and held him there. I wasn't even sure if I wanted to go back outside when I witnessed it, but we had to come to your aid. So, I made our purchases and snatched Eve out of there in hopes of rescuing you. I mean, even I know you're used to doing irrational things to get out of situations, but seeing you climb out of the back of that SUV was hilarious on top of everything. I thought you might have hurt something when you fell out the back of it and-"

"Felix is the Gaius I spoke to you of before, Sean." Eve interrupts. It looks like she knows the only way to get a word in after Herm starts up is to interrupt. "Felix, as you called him, is the one who can track us if we use our celestial energy and he won't stop for anything until he catches me. He is not a human being although he uses the appearance to blend in just as I do. This means we will have to be careful if we wish for him not to find us."

"So Felix is the one you've been telling me I have to protect you against all this time?"

"Yes. He's an unstoppable force and cannot be yielded by manmade weapons. Only an opposing force of equal nature can damage him. A battle with him full on now would not be wise," she says while turning to meet my gaze. "This is why your centering and connecting is important if you wish to stand a chance."

"Wait!" shouts Herm, "are you saying that Sean has to face off against that tank of a man who can tackle and flip SUVs for you to complete your task?"

She glances at Herman before looking back at me. "He does not have to face off against him unless we are cornered by him somehow."

"What she's saying is that if I complete my centering, I will be strong enough to tackle and flip SUVs." She nods and turns back to look out the window. Herman laughs and shakes his head in disbelief.

"You'll be the real-life Superman."

"I guess I better get back to my centering then. But before I do, I need to know why you took the time to wait in line to pay for these phones and snacks and whatnot while I was getting snatched up earlier?"

Eve grins and looks at me. "That was my doing, Sean. I couldn't risk Felix finding me just yet without a better means of protecting ourselves. You are my only hope for protection against him."

"No pressure," Herman says. "But what about your abilities, Eve? With you already being a celestial being, doesn't this mean you have what it takes to fight him off?" Good observation, Herman. I don't know why I didn't think of that myself before he mentioned it.

"My celestial energy is an extension of time and space from which I was created. I can react to others before they act, yes. This gives me more than enough speed to evade the Gaius, but I am still no match for him. As powerful as I am, I did not spend centuries hunting and battling as he has. I lack the experience. Therefore, I'm granted the ability to connect to a guardian, one who shows talent, and with a proper tutor, can be the protector we need to accomplish the task. The task is to reach the dying soul before the Gaius reaches us."

"Sounds like I better get to work then. Let's see if I can remember how to get back into this inner realm of yours." I close my eyes and sit back in the seat, still trying to come to terms with all of this.

"Quick question, Eve," Herman says. "We're passing several hospitals on the way to the one in North Carolina. What makes this life to save more important than any other?"

Eve looks at him as if the answer is obvious. "Because it's the one that fate has deemed important to the advancement of your society. I have no choice, but to comply."

"That's enough of your questions, for now, Herm. I gotta get this cosmic sh...stuff started." I say trying my best not to swear.

"Just don't let her help you because we don't need Felix showing up, and I like my vehicle to remain upright, thanks," Herman adds.

# 11.

I finally stumble out of my room after sleeping for nearly five hours. I make my way down the hallway and towards the office where I last left Samuel to complete the work I started before my slumber. No sounds are coming from the office as if no one is in there at all, but I remember how close we were to figuring out the next step to this puzzle, so I begin to step faster. Upon entering the office, I could see Samuel staring at the board with new images added to it along with labels printed on the tops of the photocopies. The TV was still on a news broadcasting channel but muted. He must have found more footage of our stargazing friend. I walk over to the coffee maker and take the pot out. It was cold and in need of refreshing. I usually have him take care of this sort of thing, but I'll tend to the pot since he has taken up the mantle for the last few hours.

"Dr. Carson, you won't believe all the sightings of this guy I found in the footage. None of the cameras got a clear shot of him, so he still seems shadowy, but it has to be the same man from last night," Samuel explains while directing my attention to the board with all his added information. "Not only is he at every single meteor shower, but he also waits at the apex of the event where the stars can be best viewed, hence the reason we are able to catch him at all the sites in our footage. It takes a survey team and crew for us to figure the apex out while he just walks up to it right before the show starts. Our cameras are running for at least an hour or two before the first sightings of fallen matter are in view."

"It's almost like he has a natural sense for these things as they occur," I reply. "Perhaps he is more than just brawn and muscle. These findings are incredible, Samuel. You've done well while I've been resting. You should be pleased."

Sam turns around and looks at me with a satisfying grin. "Doctor, there is one more thing I found about him that is vital. After finding him in all the recent years' footage, I decided to go a step further. I contacted the recording department and got access to the digitized footage, stored in the VPN, to see if he was in any of our old footage. I found the same shadowy imagery of him from over twenty years ago. What does this all mean, doctor?"

I take the coffee pot into the kitchen while rubbing my chin. My mind starts to formulate a hypothesis as Sam scurries behind me to hear what I have to say on the matter. "All I can see here is that he's been appearing at all these sites as if he is waiting on something to arrive. Maybe last night when we met him at the crash site, he was waiting for that one as well, but whatever landed there was nowhere to be found." I pour tap water into the pot as I grab a new bag of imported coffee from my cabinet. "I think we were there hoping to find the same thing, but someone either got to that goal before we did, or the goal stood up and got away on its own two feet." I make my way back into the office with my shadow of an assistant in tow and begin the coffee brewing process.

"If what you say is true, then maybe we can make the discovery of our lives in a matter of hours. Should we report to the board with all our information and see if we can track down this Felix character with the help of local law enforcement? I'm sure that we could put in a request for them to find him," Sam suggests.

I watch as the coffee begins to drip into the pot and realize I should wash out my coffee mug as well. I grab it and step out of the room and back to the kitchen. "Our research is indeed enough to get the request we need filled, but I'm not sure if he's the one we should be looking for. I feel that he too is tracking what we were tracking at the crash site." That and I'm not sure that the police are ready to handle what we came across last night. It's as if he isn't human at all.

"Dr. Carson!" Samuel shouts from the office. "You better come take a look at this". I finish cleaning my cup and make my way to the office to see Sam near the television, increasing the volume the old fashioned way. He didn't bother to find the remote under all the files and loose papers. He steps away from the TV, and I could see cell phone footage from what looks like the inside of a filling station. The footage catches what seems to be a fight outside of a gas station with a large familiar figure being the focus of the event – our current person of interest, Felix. The very same monstrosity we met last night. He ran out into the street after flipping an SUV over and watched as a late model Nissan SUV speeds down the road. He was after whatever was in that vehicle.

"It's time, Sam. First, call the Department of Transportation. Get them to put out the red alert on that SUV, stop and apprehend that vehicle, and everyone in it. Secondly, call the main office and tell them to activate the Southern region tact team. Seeing what Felix can do along with our findings is enough proof that we're on to something and may need reinforcements to contain it." Samuel peels himself away from the TV after watching the footage replay itself again and seeing Felix flip an SUV over single-handedly. He looks at me, pulls his cellphone out of his pocket, and begins scrolling through his contacts.

# 12.

The field stretches in every direction. The grass is void of color; dead as winter as far as the eye can see. In some spots, there are dirt patches. They were spotting where grass was supposed to grow but didn't. Strange colors dance across the sky, like a raging fire, and as I gaze out around me taking in all of this, there is no one else to be found. Dropping to my knees, I begin to feel the loneliness attack me, becoming so heavy, it physically weights down on my body. The feeling of being in nothingness quivers through my bones as I rub my arms for warmth in this cold place. A cold that I didn't feel until this very second.

"It's a sad sight to see, isn't it, Sean?" a voice echoes around me. "However, don't let the fear overcome you. This is all that is left of your connection to yourself and the universe. All this can still be reversed now that I am here to help you."

The voice sounds familiar, but nothing appears to be in my view.

"I'm here to help guide you as far as I can, to help you speed up the process that is necessary for you to reach the goal at hand. I'm here to help you regain yourself and re-establish your connection to the universe and its vast powers. Sean, I am here to help you become cosmic," Eve states from somewhere far away. I don't bother to look around to find her because she sounds so distant, but I finally open my eyes and see her in front of me. She is standing there, but not standing there. I could see her image clearly, yet transparently. It's as if she is a ghost. A form of herself constructed of glass. "Rise to your feet, Sean. I will show you all you need to repair the scorched and damaged lands within you, but you must act on your own will and your own behalf. I cannot make the choices for you," she says, still sounding as if to speak to me in echoes as her lips never part. I nod my head and slowly rise to my feet. "First things first, we must gain life in these barren lands."

"I get it, Eve. I'm a crappy person on the inside. No need to beat a dead horse, but I'm sure we could find one if we look a few yards away from here," I say, hiding my discomfort.

Eve shakes her head at my attempted humor and continues, "Listen carefully, to become cosmic, you must become at ease with your past. You must accept your present and be beyond it. Only then will you be able to cross the threshold and be reborn into the universe. Let us start with your past. It is the reason why life cannot flourish here, Sean. You are holding on to something that is like a poison and eats away at you. Close your eyes and find the cause of this effect."

I close my eyes and begin to reminisce. All my past is full of moments that could have led up to this. The most recent spot in my memory surfaces almost uncontrollably. I can feel a gust of wind pass me by, and just as quick as it came, it was gone. It alarms me enough to open my eyes to catch a younger, yet a freshly bruised version of myself looking down at a letter handwritten by Victoria. The letter was not to me but my wife, Jasmine. By this time, Victoria and I had slept together more times than I care to admit, and she always insisted that I leave Jasmine for her. She got fed up with me and decided to give an extra helping hand in ruining my damaged relationship. Jasmine had already punched me on her way out the door. This was the first time but not the last time I cheated on her. However, the first time is always the most important. The first time makes the rest that much easier to do. Jasmine had put up with all my mistreatment of her and managed to bear our beautiful daughter which put an end to all my dirt, but I could never get clear of it. You can always get up and dust yourself off, but the dirt will always remain. I glance over at Eve as she turns her head away from younger me.

"This may be a terrible memory for you, but this is not the source of your anguish. You must dive deeper to uncover a much darker time in your life," She commands. I close my eyes again and let my mind plummet into the past. The wind gusts across my body as I feel myself being transported through my history. It stops abruptly, and there stood a teenage me in front of a desk in an office suite downtown. My knuckles were swollen, and my muscles ached from the night before. I had just helped fight in my first mafia shakedown. I wasn't Sebastian's right hand yet. I had to work my way up to that privilege. I started where everyone else did, and that's collecting from business owners and outstanding loans alike, but I had to go out again this night. This is the night I beat up a family man in front of his wife and son. Looking back now, I could see the issue, but then I only followed orders. The whole gang was the first thing like family to me since my dad was put in a hole to rot until he died. I didn't have to look at Eve to know that I must go deeper. Once I thought of him, I knew he was the cause of this dread. I close my eyes long enough to blink, and I find myself in the house I never wanted to come back to – the house of my biological parents. I could see my drunken dad as he yells at my mother, but the adolescent me is nowhere to be found. It's because I viewed the whole incident from the pantry. I'm on the phone with the police as my dad strangles the life out of my mother. I wanted to attack him and save her, but I was too afraid. He had beaten me more times than I could count, and one thing he knew how to install into the ones around him was fear. He came after me once he killed my mom, but the cops managed to get there before he could finish the job. I hated him for making me an orphan. I hated him for beating us every chance he got, but I'm angry at myself for not stopping him sooner and not having the courage to save my mother from this monster.

"What your father did here was a heinous act, but you are not to blame. You were a child, Sean. A child does not have the power needed to overcome these circumstances, and this is the reason they must trust in their parents to make things right just as you aspire to do right with Jada," Eve proclaims.

Eve is right. I wipe my tears from the pain of reliving this moment. The pain that turned my life upside down all these years. This isn't the kind of man I want Jada to have to live with. "I hid this moment deep within myself and never wanted to remember it. Seeing it now resonates with what I've become. I can no longer let what my father did decide what kind of man I am. I can't beat myself up about the past. I'm stronger now, and I would never let Jada live the life I had to live in a gang just to feel some sort of distorted love. Never could I force her to live with anger or blame herself, and it starts with forgiving me. I know this is what made me the man I am today. This is the reason why I surrounded myself with violence and suffering, but I can't let this happen anymore and let the innocence of another child be damned," I say, feeling renewed energy. I could feel the wind pick up again around. My eyes close, and when I reopen them, I'm back in the field again, but this time the grass was green and lush all about. The sky is blue with swirls of white clouds. For once, everything feels normal.

"You did it, Sean," Eve says, "You've overcome the anger against yourself to allow growth and prosperity. I'm proud of you, and you've done well, but that is enough for one day. Just know that when you leave here, you will be in a weakened state. It's only natural when completing the first step and learning how to navigate the inner world of yourself. Goodbye for now, and when you return, we will move to the next step."

I open my eyes instantly as she finishes the sentence to find myself in the car alone outside a motel next to a Waffle House. My sight is blurred, and I feel woozy. I vomit as soon as I open the door.

# 13.

My eyes blink open to the sunlight funneling through the curtains. The room smells of stale cigarettes and fresh linen. It all starts to come back to me now. I went in too deep with my training last night, and I stumbled into the Waffle House to get a room key. Herman was in there eating dinner with Eve, and he made a remark on how deathly I looked, so I dragged myself back to the room. I could feel something radiating warmth next to me. I turn to see Eve sleeping on her back. Her expression looks even more serene while she sleeps. Across from her in the other full-size bed, I could see a lump of a body under the covers which I could only assume is Herman. For a second I wondered why she chose to rest with me, but I'm her guardian now, and she'll probably be sticking to me like glue until we get to her destination. Or maybe she didn't want to get too close to Herman. My stomach growls and I remember I had nothing to eat before crashing last night. I'm also in need of a quick shower. Scanning the room with the help of the sunlight slipping in through the curtains, I can spot my bag on top of the table. I'm happy Herman knew not to set it on the floor. No telling what kind of rodents this cheap place has slithering or crawling around.

I come out of the bathroom dressed and ready to go grab some food. I thought my hunger was going to eat me alive at one point during my shower. The feeling of fatigue from the mental activities has vanished completely for now, and I never felt better. In fact, I feel more energized and vibrant as ever. The other two have not so much as moved since I went into the shower. I tip past them as fast as I could and make a silent exit. The sunlight against my face made my eyes squint, but the feeling of it on my skin is different. I could feel and see everything clearer or more intimately. Today is the first day I felt like smiling with no real reason in mind as I stroll out of the parking lot to get my breakfast next door. Glancing in through the glass, there were maybe six or seven people already in there. I can see a man just enjoying his morning coffee as he reads the paper. Across from his table is a couple sitting side by side, the man holding his chubby brunette girlfriend as the waitress sits the food on their table. I'm just going to have a seat in the back booth and just take in this new feeling about life I have flowing through me.

"Good morning, sir. Can I get you something to drink while you look at the menu?" Asks the same waitress I just saw at the couple's table. She has dark eyes and blue streaks in her bleach blonde hair. I glance at the menu, but I already know what I want.

"I'll take an omelet, bacon, a stack of pancakes, and an orange juice, please," I respond without delay. She nods and writes it all down on a slip of paper.

"It'll be right out for ya, sir. I'll get that orange juice now," she says with a smile and walks away. There is an old model TV hanging down from the ceiling a few tables from me, but it's in my direct line of sight with the volume turned high enough to hear parts of the news over the diner music that regularly plays in places like these. It currently says something about the weather with the local meteorologist giving his best-educated guess at the weather for the rest of the weekend. Judging by the rate at which we're going now, we should be at the Evergreen Hospital late tonight or early morning tomorrow without any delays. I should venture back into myself to complete all the training, but it'll be after I eat, and once we get back on the road again. Time seems to fly by when I'm there, and it's a great excuse for skipping my turn to drive today. I wait patiently while taking in the music of the diner and eying the television.

ARUBA, JAMAICA, OHH I WANNA TAKE YA.

BUMUTA. BAHAMA. COME ON PRETTY MAMA...

I could see it now. Sorry, Herman, but I can't drive because I'm still trying to develop my inner superpowers so that we can protect Eve from what is to come. The waitress drops off the juice with a straw and speeds off to get another table. I sip the orange juice and spot a young officer looking at me through the window of the restaurant from the outside. His glance could've been him mistaking me for someone else, but given my history with officers, I'd have to say otherwise. He lit up a cigarette and attempts to stand there unassumingly. The diner music begins to fade away to transition to the next track. The anchorman could be heard clearly from the television.

"The votes seem to keep pouring into the station even after the city has already decided to change the date of the fair arriving into town, so we decided to…"

Maybe my suspicions are getting the best of me. Maybe he is just taking a smoke before coming in and ordering some coffee with his donuts. My food comes right on time to ease my paranoia and end my hunger. I begin to devour my breakfast feast, ignoring everything around me other than the overture.

OHH. OH. OH.OH. FOR THE LONGEST TIME.

OH. OH. OH. OH. FOR THE LONGEST TIME.

My mind wanders back to another problem at hand, and that's the fact that Viktor and his gang are still after me. Learning how to accept my past won't be the answer I need to deal with them, and they won't believe anything I say about not killing their boss's brother. I can't think of another way to handle them that wouldn't pay homage to the old me; that won't end in bloodshed.

"..concerning that incredible video that's been circulating everywhere, police ask you all to be on the lookout for one of the individuals that are believed to be a part of the…"

"Here's your check, sir," the waitress says as she sits it on the table. I see the total and grab twenty bucks out of my pocket, placing it on top of the check before she has a chance to leave.

"Keep the change," I mumble after taking a big gulp of orange juice to wash down the food. She smiles and takes my plate, and that's when I see it; a mugshot of me on the screen, along with footage of me jumping into Herman's car outside the gas station yesterday. Someone must have filmed the whole thing with their cell phone. They even got a blurry image of Felix flipping the SUV over with his bare hands. I don't know which was worse: watching him flip that truck over like a toy knowing that he's after us or being pursued by the police? Wait. I turn my head to look at the cop that was standing outside and notice that he never came in at all. I couldn't see any squad cars outside yet, but I'm sure he recognized me.

Making my way towards the door, I could see the chubby girl with her boyfriend staring at me. She probably caught that picture of the criminal at large on the screen. I hit the exit to the restaurant and try to move quickly but casually. Something doesn't add up about me being "wanted." I didn't commit any of the violence in the video, and I wasn't the one who flipped a vehicle over onto two other people. And I seriously doubt they'll ever catch Felix because they wouldn't be able to tame him.

"Excuse me, sir," the voice behind me says while I was scurrying. "I'm going to need you to come with us." I turn to see the officer from earlier along with his partner this time. All this could have been avoided if I had simply ordered in.

"Officers, I'm sure this is just one big misunderstanding. I haven't done anything wrong here," I plea to them knowing that it never works. "I'm just passing through, and I won't be of any more trouble to you if…"

"We can't let you go, sir. Just cooperate, and if everything checks out when we get down to the station, we won't have to hold you up any longer than we have to, so just come along," he says as he places a hand on his taser. I turn my head away and glance at my nearest escape which would be the middle of nowhere behind this hotel, but then I spot a few onlookers. Herman is one of them staring at me, not even a bit surprised about the situation.

"Where is the station, officers? I really have to be somewhere, and I can't afford to lose any ground. Isn't there some way you guys can just ask what you need to ask right now?" I try my hand again at bargaining with them. This is classic criminal 101: try to talk your way out of it while not actually talking your way but looking for a means of escape. The older cop face wrinkles up into a frown. It seems he knows what's about to happen next. He's been around long enough to tell when my tactic is taking root. He draws his taser before the young cop does.

"We don't want to have to hurt you, sir, just get into the car." The older cop says in a heightened voice. He's done playing this game, and I still don't have a way out of this without confrontation. Looks like it's time to see how much my power has increased since completing the first step yesterday.

A metallic click sounds off.

Suddenly, my body goes stiff with a surge of electricity pulsing through it. I couldn't stop myself from falling backward onto the warm pavement. The pulses stop, and my vision of the crowd comes back. There stands Eve, next to Herman among the other random pedestrians watching in awe. Most people have never seen anything like this in person. The cop tries to roll me over on my back, and without thinking, I resist, grabbing his ankle and shoving it forward with more strength than I planned to use. He smashes painfully against the pavement next to me but not painful enough for him to stay put. The young officer rolls away from me as I begin to fill the surges pulse through my body again but for a longer duration this time.

"Try that again, and I'll tase you until you're unconscious!" the veteran cop shouts. My body recovered amazingly fast from the surges, but I didn't want to be knocked unconscious. And just like that, I feel the all too familiar feeling of handcuffs around my wrist and the smell of the back of a cop car –the scent of old leather and sweat. Just like old times.

Welcome back, Hammer.

# 14.

"Hi. You've reached Jasmine. I'm unable to get to the phone right now, but if you would leave a message with your number, I'll be more than happy to return your call. Thanks for calling and have a great day. BEEP."

"Listen, Jazzy. I know you probably hate my guts right now, but I had to call you to let you know that I miss you and Jada very much. If you've seen me on the news, you can see that I got myself mixed up in something that looks a lot like my old antics. Baby, you gotta believe me when I say it's different this time. I don't have a lot of time to explain to you what all this is about, but know I love you both and I'll be back soon to tell you about..."

BEEP.

The timer on the voicemail cut the rest of my message off unforgivingly. I called her twice from the payphone, and I could see the officer sitting at his desk getting uneasy as he watches me. He looks to have an amused grin on his round face. The nameplate on his desk reads, "Chief Murphy," so he's the one that runs the show around here. Unlike the cops that brought me in, Murphy here is wearing a cheap gray suit with his belly hiding his waistline. A feature I'm sure he acquired from years of donuts and coffee shops.

"Time to get off the phone, sir," he shouts over my frustration. "You're only allowed one call, and I let you give it a few tries. Sounds like you got yourself a woman who doesn't want to be bothered by you no more," he mocks with a country accent.

I cringe and stop myself from acting irrationally to avoid another set of taser cables attaching to my mid-section. "She's not done with me yet, but she has put up with me for far too long. Hopefully, she gets my message and can get in touch with my lawyers." Murphy snorts lightly at my comment. I say nothing as I slowly hang up the phone, taking in the fact that I'm in handcuffs yet again in my life, but I wasn't sure why this time. Most times are clear cut. Either I slapped some guys around or was accused of arson of private property. For the first time, I was legitimately the victim in the footage that aired on the news earlier this morning. The video showed that outright.

"Escort him to his cell, Officer Kelly," the chief orders the younger cop that arrested me earlier. You can tell that he was still new at his job by his nervousness but determined to make a good impression on his superiors. He places a hand on my shoulder and points to a door opposite the entrance they escorted me in through. It goes right past the chief's desk, and I'm thinking this will probably be the last time I get to talk to him for a while, so I'm going to get the answers I need now. Kelly gets me as far as his desk, and I stop my stride.

"Chief Murphy, I have a simple question," I speak humbly, knowing that's the best approach to his type. "Why am I under arrest? It's a question for my lawyer to handle, but I don't think you really have any grounds to lock me up."

"Well, think again, boy. Not only were you involved in some kind of freak event that sent three guys to the ER, but I think you have a lot more to do with this than you let on."

"I'll tell you like I told your troopers; I was minding my own business when these guys pursued me violently. Even the footage shows that they were armed as I was making my escape from them. I'm the victim and not the suspect. This just doesn't make sense to me."

"You make a valid argument there, but the Department of Transportation wants you on lockdown until they are able to get someone out here to question you specifically. I don't know why and hell, I don't care. I just know that they wanted you behind bars as soon as we found you and now, here we are. Get him out of here, Kelly," Murphy barks as he tosses his feet on top of his desk and lounges back in his seat. Kelly gives me a stern shove, and we're back on our way to the holding cells. The police station isn't a very big one. It has just enough space for few desks and some cells to hold someone in before hauling them away into one of the major city prisons unless the person arrested had some way of making bail before they could transport them. On the way in, I could see them building a bigger station outside. The two buildings were already connected with a halfway done hallway missing sheetrock and the works.

Once through the doors leading to the holding cell, the smell of bleach and old piss hit me like no other. The holding area is even smaller than the office, considering there is only a short hallway and a total of four holding cells all next to each other. The only thing across the hallway from the cells was a room for a guard to be stationed with a lookout window to view all the prisoners from the desk. Kelly slides the cell door open and points at me to go in. I hold up my hands for him to take off the cuffs and he shakes his head in disagreement before shoving me inside. I stumble inside off balance as I hear the cell door clatter shut.

"The DOT representative shouldn't be much longer, and you'll have to be in handcuffs when they come to speak to you. No need to remove them now just to put them back on, right," the young officer says with a grin. "Besides, you made me look bad in front of my trainer out there today, so this should make it even. Sit tight, Mr. Sean. We'll be with you in a little bit. There's a toilet there in the far corner of the cell, and you can pick any four of the bunk beds here to rest your head. The sheets are fresh I think, but if you see any vomit stains on it, I would avoid them." He smiles and makes his way back out into the office. Walking over to the bed, I give the cell a once over. The cement floor is old and dingy from stains of the past. The toilet is in the open next to a small sink that both look to be a rusty and stained, tarnished and battered. I make it in front of the bed and see clean white linen sheets. The pillowcase used to be white at some point, but now it's more stained yellow. I sit under the shade of the bunk bed from the bright fluorescent light above the cell. It's so much brighter in here than it was in the office — a tactic for discomfort, most likely.

Jasmine wouldn't come for me here. She's been involved in one too many of my lockups. A price I paid heavily for being Hammer. My last hope is for Herman and Eve to show up and get me out of this somehow. Maybe they made the hard choice and continued to the hospital without me, but something tells me they haven't yet.

\*\*\*

We pull into the police station, ready to take on the task at hand.

Now it normally takes an act of Congress to get us in motion but given the recent events that just happened a little over twenty-four hours ago, it's clear that something else is at play here. I climb out of the back of the armored transport and grab my M4 from the seat next to me, attaching it to the combat sling, holstered to my chest.

"This is the shittiest looking police station I've ever laid eyes on, boss," Michelle spits as she climbs out of the driver seat. She pushes down the sunglasses from the top of her freshly buzzed dark hair to shield her eyes from the afternoon sun. She makes her way around the truck, and I could hear the snapping of her rifle attaching to her holster. She stands next to Reese as he situates his gear and gives him a quick look over as he does.

"I don't know, Shell. It is quite the shithole, but I think it's better for us and our mission this way. Look on the bright side: if anything does go wrong and this is a code blue or green, we could always shoot our way out of it with fewer casualties and even fewer-"

"Witnesses," I finish. Well, the situation is as follows, the tact team. I got a report verifying we have a key witness to some phenomenon that occurred yesterday. Our plan is to go in, secure the area before the rest of the team can arrive and get the answers from the witness about the target. Judging from Dr. Carson's research, the prisoner either knows what the target wants and where to find it or he is the target's agenda. In either case, we confirm this before the doctor shows up to make things run quickly and smoothly. That means we get the information by any means necessary. You copy?" Reese nods and begins to make his way to the doors of the station while Shell looks at me with a grin.

"I always love it when we get to play before the stiffs show up, but you already know that, Marcus."

I smile at her. "Let's keep the torture shit to a minimum this time."

# 15.

My senses finally start to wrap themselves around the impurities of the jail after an hour. My mind finally stops racing, and I'm finally able to relax enough to remember that I'm more than the average human now. I should take this time now to complete some inner training and establish that connection Eve told me about. This would be a fine time to develop any superhuman abilities. I'll do just as Eve taught me. Close my eyes, relax, and focus on my inner self. Minutes begin to pass as I feel my environment around me shift. My eyes peel open, and I see lush green fields and fully-grown trees. I could feel a faint breeze against my skin, refreshing my senses, and causing goosebumps.

"You did excellent for the first step, Sean. It was even rather surprising," Eve's clear image says, standing next to me as if she was there the whole time. "You are purging yourself of all the anger and hatred of your past, and you did it quicker than I could have anticipated. The next step, however, will be a little different and a lot harder to grasp, but I'm confident you will not allow yourself to be defeated here in your universe."

I dust myself off arrogantly and smirk. "Thanks, Eve. Things like this wouldn't be possible if you weren't here to help me with it. And yes, you're right. I'm not going to let anything stop me from reaching my full potential for you."

Eve's facial expression never changes, but I could somehow feel her disapproval. "Reaching your true potential is not only for our safety, but it's also ultimately for you and the future, Sean. Always remember that above all else. Our next step is to turn our attention to your atmosphere." She points up to the sky that is dark with fiery red clouds. The clouds are so thick and clustered together that I can see the sun rays shining through the small gaps of nothingness in between. I never paid the sky much attention until now. "Now, Sean, you'll have to face your present to move on to the next step of the connection. With this you…" She stops mid-sentence.

"What's wrong, Eve?" I question as she looks off into the distance.

"Something is happening that I didn't prepare for and this could be quite a problem to the plan." I look at her puzzled as I stare off in the same direction as her and see nothing. "You should know that we're on our way to retrieve you. We thought to leave without you, but I can't leave my guardian behind."

"I thought I would be mad about you not moving forward, but I'm relieved you guys are coming back. I know I can be a bit of a handful with all my problems, but I appreciate everything."

She finally turns her attention back to me. "For now, you have company, and they can be ruthless, so tread carefully around them. Try not to use any of your- "

I awake with pain radiating from my back. I remember sitting on the bed before and now I'm on my back against the cold cement floor, looking up at a woman in brown and tan fatigues. Her hair is buzzed down to almost nothing, and I would have thought of her to be a man if her breast weren't there.

"Don't you hear me talking to you, clown?" she asks as she glares down at me. "We have a few things to ask you, and the faster you answer the questions, the easier this can be for us all."

I look out into the hallway and see two men looking at us, wearing the same uniform she's in, but they have weapons strapped to their chest. I sit up and look at her before I respond. "Relax, lady. I'll be sure to answer any questions you have for me. Now I'm no interrogator, but shouldn't you give me a chance to answer something before you get physical?"

She smiles down at me and takes a few steps away, walking to the jail bars. "You weren't responsive to anything at all before, so I nudged your ass. Sometimes I don't know my own strength." I say nothing as I take my seat on the bed. I've dealt with cops on both sides of the law before, and I don't think they're cops at all. "Well, boss, I think he's ready for you." The man walks up to the bars with a hand tracing his trimmed mustache and beard as if he was revving himself up. His hair is black and slick back carefully with a light coat of hair gel.

"Alright, Sean, my name is Captain Marcus, and we're actually from a government-sanctioned organization dealing with matters beyond human comprehension. I have a few questions to ask you before the scientist arrives, and I don't want you to make this more difficult than it has to be, so listen carefully and respond accordingly with a yes, no, or a direct answer to the question I present. No fuck around games," the boss says calmly. Something tells me he's more than just a pretty boy. I look over at the female soldier standing against the bars of my cell. She smirks at me and shifts her head as if to direct my attention to her boss.

"We saw the footage from many angles from the gas station, and we need to know exactly what we're getting ourselves into. Seeing how your mafia friends are in critical condition and not able to give the authorities answers, you'll have to talk. How are you connected with them?"

"Are you kidding me? Mafia? I had no idea those guys were in the mafia. They only asked me for directions before things got blown out of proportion," I reply with a straight face.

"Cute. Real cute," says the man standing outside the cell with his arms crossed over his weapon as if he was hugging it.

"He's lying, and you know what we do to liars, Shell," he says as he gives her an approving nod. She dashes across the room and punches me square in the jaw. Pain rushes across my cheekbone. A pain that I'm very familiar with. Not too bad a hit for a woman. However, just as quickly as it happened, the pain was gone. I blinked and looked at her with a stun expression on my face to keep the façade going.

"Unlikely for a cop to hit their suspect, so I'm guessing you freaks aren't cops. Where's Officer Kelly or whoever? At least he warned me before he zapped me!" I yell at them.

"Cats out the bag, folks," the boss says between laughs, "We aren't here to read you your rights or even act like you have rights at this point, shitbag. We're here to get answers. Now, a man that can flip a fucking six-ton truck over like it's a damn toy is after you. We're here to find out where he comes from, how and, what you know about him."

I couldn't hide the fact that they know he's something more than some roided out, muscle head. "If you want answers about him, you're asking the wrong guy."

"You're lying. He's after you for a reason, Sean, and I'm not sure why you are protecting him, but you are going to give us the information we need the easy way or the easier way," says the boss as he nods to Shell for another session of abuse. She punches me twice followed by a roundhouse kick that knocks me off the bed. The pain lasts longer than it did before, and I end up spitting blood from my mouth. When the pain stops, my mind was already made up. I was trying to prevent them from having to encounter Felix, but they wanted him. I'll have to lead him here somehow with my newfound power and hope to be able to escape from everything in the confusion. I'm trying my luck yet again, but that's when I do my best work. I lift myself off the ground, wiping my mouth as I do and look the boss dead in his eyes.

"Fine, you win. I'll tell you what I know about this guy. I'll even do you a solid and get him to come this way if you give me the time I need." I watch as his anger-filled expression changes to one full of surprise and excitement. I said exactly what he wanted to hear.

# 16.

I give them the whole spill that Eve told me about Felix. Seeing how they are a part of some elite tactical force that specializes in activities that are unclear to normal standards like the one that happened yesterday, it shouldn't sound so farfetched to them. The whole time, Shell looks like she wants to knock me around more, but their boss or captain keeps her under control. I was able to read their nametapes and get their names while I spoke. They have me cornered in this cage, and they are heavily armed. Now wasn't the time to try anything that could potentially get me killed?

"So you're saying that this guy is something made by Earth and is here to protect us from galactic danger," the Captain responds to my lengthy statement. I told them all I knew about Felix but nothing about Eve or what we are up to. "So, if he's after you, doesn't that mean you're the threat he wants to end?"

"You would think that was the case, but if I was the threat, Captain, do you think I would be in here letting your, ahem, personnel beat up on me if I was some kind of alien thing?"

"So why is he after you at all, Sean? You have something he wants. What are you hiding from us?" the captain asks me relentlessly.

"I can bring him here so you can ask him all the questions you want, Marcus. I just need rest to do so. He and I have some kind of connection that he picks up on whenever I concentrate long enough. I can lead him here, and you can take him into custody or ask him all the questions you want, and hopefully, he doesn't kill us all first," I inform him, but he doesn't seem like the type to let a challenge slip through his fingers. Looking at Shell, she was skeptical about the whole thing. I don't know if my story sounded too strange for her to believe or was she in fear about what kind of trouble this could cause for them?

Maybe she realizes that bringing Felix here would be the end of us all. His man from earlier comes running back into the room along with the police chief of the station.

"Did the rest of the men get here as we requested, Reese?" Marcus questions his subordinate, waiting for a definite answer to his liking.

"Yes, sir," Reese confirms his captain's hopes. "All the men we requested are on site, and I put them in place to secure the area as you ordered. Nothing should be able to get in or out without us knowing. Put a total perimeter lockdown on everything other than the police chief here. He has demanded to stay on site until this whole ordeal is done."

"This station is my life, and I don't need you or your men ransacking it especially with the new add-on construction going on. Besides, I want to be a part of the capture of this unknown man. Another notch on my belt."

"Suit yourself, chief. However, as long as we're here, I'm in control, and we don't need you here with the prisoner now, so if you could get back to your duties at your desk, that would be most helpful. I'm sure your patrolling officers still need some guidance," the captain says as he points back towards the entryway of the holding area. The chief looks as if he is a child being scolded by his favorite teacher, but he does just as he asked of him and heads towards the door.

"What's the estimated time of arrival for the doctor, Reese?"

"He should be here within the hour, captain."

Captain Marcus looks down at his watch before our eyes connect. "Alright then, Sean, looks like you're on. I'll give you some undisturbed time to get him here. If the doctor cannot confirm this method of communication with his research or if you don't deliver, you're going to have a fucking bad day. Also, if you are just trying to buy time for whatever reason, that will make for a bad fucking day for you."

I stare into Marcus's blue eyes and scoff. "Apparently, you don't know me very well. The last few years of my life have been nothing but a series of bad days, so don't threaten me with a good time. I'll get to work and bring him to you now." I look up at Shell with a puzzled look across my face. "I don't think you have to be in here to slap me around anymore, missy. We've come to an agreement." Before she could respond, I turn my head back to Marcus and say, "Get this man thing out of my cell. I can't concentrate with all that testosterone in here."

"You dumb shit!" She raises her hand to punch me again.

"Michelle!" shouts Reese to stop her mid punch. "Captain has everything he needs for now. We need him conscious if we want to get our man." Her anger instantly subsides with a deep exhale. She settles with a shove of my face and exits the cell.

"This ain't over. Once you do what you agreed, you'll be seeing me again."

"I'm looking forward to it since our first encounter was just so heartwarming," I reply.

Just like that, all of them have left the holding area. They placed someone at the watchmen's desk to make sure I didn't try to chew my way through the bars or dig out of here. I splash my face with some water from the sink and rub my jawbones with my hands still in cuffs. I couldn't feel pain or see any bruises on my face. Completing the first step has worked more than I could imagine and now it's time to do the second. Somehow, I'm going to have to get Felix to come in this direction. Eve said not to use my abilities, and he'll never be able to pinpoint me, but I'm banking everything on the next step. Hopefully, I'll be able to complete it and open some new kind of power that can get Felix's attention, or I'll have to fend for myself with another run-in with Michelle, aka Betty Bruiser. I get myself together and take my seat on the bed with my back against the wall. I close my eyes in silence and begin to feel the inner power of the connection again.

I open my eyes, and I'm back in the field. I take a few steps to get my ground, peering into the distance of an incomplete connection that lies within me. I don't have a lot of time to spare here, so I have to get this over with soon.

"You've come back. I'm happy to see that," Eve says as she forms out of thin air right before my eyes. Her body still transparent just as the last time we met here. "Now I heard your plan to call out to Felix. I don't think that's wise, but it is all you have left for now. Herman and I are on the way for you. Hopefully, we can get to you before you do something brash. You may think that this is a good plan, but I'm sure he won't be so willing to let you go as freely as he did before, Sean."

"I figured he would be a little angrier than our first meet. That's okay, Eve. Maybe I'll be able to keep up with him with a little help from the universe, huh?"

She falls silent to thoughts of the possibility of me facing off against Felix. "Completing the next step will increase your bond tremendously, but you will still be incomplete. As long as you are, you will stand no chance against a Gaius."

"Have a little faith in me, Eve. I've been against the odds before, and I'm not saying I'll be able to kill him or anything, but I should be able to fend him off long enough for us to make a calculated escape."

"Please, don't count on that, Sean. You do him an injustice by underestimating his power." She waits for me to reply, but I remain silent. "Close your eyes and let us continue completing your connection."

I open my eyes to my apartment back in the city. It's in the same shape I left it in after fighting Viktor's men but with a few additions to the damaged table on the floor. I walk across the room to see a picture frame smashed and glass all over the living room floor. That 8x10 framed the picture that Felix flashed to me during the gas station encounter. The photo that I stuffed back into my pocket after he threw it at my feet. "What are we doing here in my apartment, Eve?" I ask her.

"You've made your way to the present, Sean. You must learn to let go and accept the life you live now. This is a place with all your belongings and things that mean much to you here. How do you feel about losing these things you worked so hard to gather?"

"I used to take a lot of value in everything I bought and owned, but not anymore. These things of mine can be stolen or lost, and I wouldn't care much about having them back."

"What of the hard work it took for you to get all your things? Does it bother you to know that it was all in vain?" Eve says to probe deeper.

"Truth is, I earned everything here mostly with my own two hands. I kept myself out of trouble and even got a legit job to make it all work. My lifestyle now is nothing like it used to be and that's because I no longer want to earn money with bloodshed. Saying this still adds no real value to any of the things I own here. The place could burn down today, and there is no part of it I would shed a tear for."

"It's good to know you are willing to let go of things that are bound to the physical plain. Another reason I'm proud of you for being who you are and the way you think about life after being in so much trouble and causing so much pain to others."

The environment of my apartment fades away slowly and is replaced by total darkness. "This next part may be hard for you to watch, but you have to be able to control your emotions and come to terms with what is happening. I won't be here to help you find the answers. You have to be able to carry this weight on your own, Sean," she says as she turns her back and walks away into the darkness. In the blink of an eye, I appear in a house that I'm very familiar with. It's the house I bought my wife and child to live in while I get my life together and earn their forgiveness. I step away from the front door and down the hallway when I see Jada looking up at someone, smiling as big as she could before she is lifted into the air and then twirled around by none other than Kevin. His face is partially swollen from the beaten I gave him yesterday morning, but he wore it with a smile. I round the corner and see them all in full view. Jasmine is sitting at the kitchen island and looking at them spin with those light eyes. Looking closer, I could see the look she used to give me back in our high school years. I can tell that she is starting to fall in love with this man.

"What the hell is going on here, Jasmine? I leave for a few hours, and you're giving this guy the look it took me years to get?" I shout at her, charging straight for her, but she doesn't move a muscle. She doesn't even turn in my direction to acknowledge me, and that's when I noticed none of them did. I discover that I'm in some type of ghost form watching them from my meditation point. "This can't be happening right now," I say to myself as I start to feel sick.

"This is happening at this very moment while you are in prison," Eve explains without making a physical appearance. "They won't be able to hear you nor will they be able to see you and vice versa. What will happen to you if you lose them, Sean? What will become of you then?" I say nothing while I watch Kevin hold my daughter in his arms. He smiles at her as if she is his very own and makes his way right over to Jasmine. She looks him in the eyes with the same passion she had for me years ago and kisses him. I scream at the top of my lungs with rage.

"That's not the correct form of action to take, but you're welcome to come back and try again when you are ready to face this task. For now, you must part with this step," Eve states faintly.

I wake sitting up in my cell as the vomit begins to erupt from my mouth. I dash for the toilet and finish throwing up. I feel sick and mad at the same time. Another man taking my family is already hard for me to imagine, but seeing it brings the pain to another level. Even thinking about it now brings me a feeling of sickening despair. Not only that, but how am I going to complete this next step successfully and get Felix here like I told the captain I would?

My only hope is to keep trying.

# 17.

"What's the status report on Sean, Reese? It's been an hour, and there is no sign of our target showing up here yet. I'm starting to think our guy is bluffing or has some other meaning for making us wait," I say as I watch the scientist adjust his suit outside the station windows.

"Well, from what I can see, boss, he's definitely going through something in there. He sits in some kind of trance for a few minutes before he vomits. He said he's reaching out to the target, but the distance is making him nauseous. I'm no expert on the matter, and I haven't been around as long as you, but Sean could pass for some kind of junkie that needs his drug fix. Maybe we can get some enlightenment on the matter from the good doctor," Reese says with a laugh.

"Don't underestimate him. The good doctor is the reason we're involved in this shit storm. He makes more money than our salaries combined by looking for these damn anomalies, so maybe he sees something we don't. He's the genius here. We'll stick to being the muscle and let men like him be the brain," I say right before the doctor opens the door and walks into the building. He's accompanied by his assistant and protégé. He's a short guy. Both of them in their poorly-tailored, dark color suits. The doctor himself has on a tie that doesn't quite match the color, while his assistant looks to be more in tune with style.

"I didn't know I was walking into a fortress, Captain. Is all this necessary to keep the prisoner in or for keeping something out?"

"It's for both, Doctor Carson. I didn't want to explain the situation until you got here and a sensitive situation it is. As you know, we manage to catch the man that escaped in the video with the help of the local law enforcement. Secondly, we couldn't get any information about the men that have been put in the hospital because of the event. I don't think they have any relevance to the situation you were researching. What we did discover is that the man chasing the prisoner here name is…"

"Felix. I ran into him a couple of days ago while looking over a crash site, and I couldn't get a lock on him then, but after the research, my assistant and I have put together, I know now that he knows much about space, time, and even the planet itself. Can I speak with the prisoner now, Captain Marcus?" The doctor asks as his eyes wander around the room, surveying the small police station office.

"I can show you where he is, but you probably won't be able to communicate with him," I say as we start towards the holding area. "He gave us a spill about Felix being some planetary guardian and how they are connected somehow. He said that if we give him some time, he can connect with him through deep concentration and get him here for us." I open the door to the holding cells, and the doctor speeds pass me.

"Connected to the guardian, he says," the doctor repeats as he stands in front of Sean's cell. Michelle comes out of the monitoring room and stands outside of the door with an eerie look on her face. Dr. Carson just stares at Sean through the bars. He is now sitting, looking out at us with his back against the far wall and resting next to the toilet. His face pale and stressed. "Now I see that you are preparing in the event of Felix making an appearance. That explains your unit being all over the place. What exactly is your plan once Felix arrives, Captain Marcus?"

"I read your report about how the target could possibly be in some kind of armor, so we have the right ammunition to put him down if he doesn't comply to come with us voluntarily. I want all my men to go home today, no matter the cost."

"Killing him puts our research back at square one. Let's hope it doesn't come to that level of violence. Take him any way possible, but we need him alive if we're going to get any more information that could complete my calculations and theories. Do not use deadly force on him."

Just like a scientist to care more about his work than the preservation of human life.

We drove past the police station without causing any suspicion before parking out here along the highway. Eve says that Sean is in there, but I don't know why they have the entire place on lockdown like he's some high-profile criminal. Even the dirt of his past doesn't warrant him to be this dangerous. "Looking from here, Eve, I don't see a way to get in undetected. Maybe you can use just a little bit of your power to get us in there and back out with Sean in tow?" Eve looks over at me from the corner of her eyes and then focuses back on the heavily guarded building.

"My power usage is a last resort. If Felix were to detect me here now, he'd surely be able to destroy us with ease."

"What's the point of being this celestial being if you can't use any of your powers, Eve? I'm sure you have more at your disposal than just life preservation and getting inside of people's minds. I mean sure, I have seen Felix do some inhuman shit, but didn't the universe give you powers to match or overcome his abilities? I would say you got the short end of the st-"

"No, Herman," she interrupts. It's as I said before; it is not that I lack the power that he does. He has been a Gaius for many moons now, and his experience dealing with celestials are way beyond my level of combative. I can't face off against him and hope to survive without Sean."

"Now I'm beginning to connect the dots here. You need Sean and his experiences as a fighter to be able to handle Felix. Now what if he wasn't a fighter, Eve? What if he was more like me?" I question her, but she falls silent. "I'm starting to think your meeting with Sean in those woods was more than just mere chance. I feel like you've been planning this all along."

"I think we can get in through the incomplete portion of the building, Herman," she says, avoiding my statement completely. "We must hurry because I fear that Sean will do something he's not ready to handle concerning his connection." She pauses before continuing to say "I didn't handpick Sean to be my guardian, Herman. The disconnected ones always assume that they have control over what time, fate, and the universe has already foreseen. Every moment we exist has a purpose. I am unsure of everyone else's purpose, but I know

74

that Sean is fated for a much different outcome than any of us."

*** 

Being within myself and suffering like this is far more exhausting than I could ever imagine. I lay in the field within, looking up at the sky. It begins to lose its red tint of all my failed attempts and the clouds begin to dissipate, revealing a clear night sky. After watching my family go on without me as if I didn't exist was the hardest thing to take, but I know now what must be done and I know that through all my errors.

"You're amazing, Sean. You were able to clear the second step of the connection. What did you learn and how did you overcome the pain?" Eve's voice whispers to me.

"I learned that my family is a great part of what I do in my life, but it's not what makes me whole. I must be able to do that myself. I know I have wronged Jasmine more times than I can count, and I have to accept the fact that I've lost her in doing just that, but I'm fine with it. She's happy again, and so is Jada. She deserves someone that is truly all for her and her mother. They both seem so happy, and the reason is that I'm not there to torture their emotions. I've learned to let them grow in happiness to achieve peace for them and myself."

"A very profound look on things. I can't believe how far you've come along so quickly. It's as if you were meant to be connected. Now I suggest you rest before you move any further."

Lifting myself off the ground and up to my feet, I bypass her warnings. "I can't stop here now, Eve. I can see the stars shining from above as the murkiness of the clouds fades away. I can feel the power beginning to surge through my body and soul. It's like a weight has been lifted and I can fly. It's like I have been holding myself back for so long, and now the chains are breaking free. I know you won't approve, but I'm going to lure Felix here and finish this once and for all. We have enough things to worry about. We have a small group of armed men with weapons here, and now that I'm connected, I can take the fight to him."

She grabs my arms and squeezes them tightly. I didn't know she could touch me in her ghostly form here in my universe. "Sean, you have to listen to me. I know you feel empowered and that you think you can handle everything that comes at you now, but this is where we go wrong. Your connection is not completed, and no matter who sides with us at this point, we are no match for him right now. With you consuming so much energy to achieve the second step, you are in a much weaker state. Because of this, if you face him now, he is sure to kill you."

I can feel the weakness she is referring to, but I can also feel the power growing within me. A power that I've never felt before. "Let me handle things from here, Eve. I'm a lot tougher than you think and now is the time. I'm not counting on these soldiers to help take him down, but I can use them as a distraction to assist in the action. He's going to take the bait, and I'll take care of him once and for all. I can feel that you are somewhere close to me outside of here, and if you don't want to be a part of this, I understand. This next-level connection is just what I needed." I turn from her and walk away into the lush field of green towards the clearing in the sky. Although the field is lit as if the sun is shining down on it, I see a night starry sky. Nothing can stand in my way.

# 18.

"How much more time do you think he needs in there? It's like he's been detoxing this whole time with all the vomiting and the moaning. I'm starting to think he's just some random druggy from off the street," says Reese to Sam as he stares at the man in his jail cell. "I've seen your research and all of it adds up, but I'm still trying to find where this junkie comes in at. It's been almost two hours, and there hasn't been any sign of the target."

I look over my shoulder to see my assistant looking through the file that we brought which includes all the sightings of Felix. Sam looks up at the soldier and then back down at the file we put together. He sighs and goes on to say, "You see all this research Dr. Carson and myself have been so focused on? Believe it or not, this didn't happen overnight. You would have no idea what we are looking for if it wasn't for us going through all the camera footage from years ago. All these moments through time caught on camera have led us up to this very point and waiting two hours is the least of our concerns here, Reese. This is a matter of world security, and if there is something out there that can turn our whole way of living upside down, then we must be patient. Better to be safe than sorry that the world imploded because we didn't react fast enough due to leaving our only lead to rot in a small-town jail and our mark got away because we were impatient. We take our work very seriously here, and if you do the same, you'll be a good soldier and follow the last direct order that has been given to you."

Reese looks down at Sam with a clenched jaw and stomps out of the watchman's office. I never heard Samuel snap back at someone like that before. He's been assisting me long enough to adopt my sharp tongue and reasoning. Nothing matters more to us than this research, and we aren't willing to risk years of dedication to the impatience of a lackey of sorts. Not sure where our human resources in my agency were finding these men, but I guess we can't be picky, knowing what they signed up to face off against which is anything under the sun that we monitor. I watch Sam as he passes Michelle out by the cell just as something glimmers from within it. Everyone stops in their tracks to investigate the prisoner. I could hear Sam ask me something, but I focus on the faint glow instead. Soon after, Sam was standing next to me, peering out through the glass. Same as I am. That's when I notice I've been holding my breath; lost in my fascination of the moment.

\*\*\*

This place still has a lot of construction to be done, and it worked out in our favor. Eve and I were able to slip in through a large window on the second floor. I'm still sweating from climbing the connexes alongside the building to reach the window. Looking down from this platform in the rafters, I could see the place littered with more construction equipment with pallets of flooring tiles and 2x4s. There is even a dusty, 4 door pickup truck and some type of mini Bobcat dozer inside the place. I can see Eve climbing down the platform carefully and precise not to make a sound and not to fall. The latter getting down from here appeared to be improvised and I'm not the most physical person in the world, but I know I don't want to fall from this thing either. It probably wouldn't kill me, but it could do some major damage depending on the angle of the fall.

"Eve," I whisper loudly, "You sure you don't want to use your space powers to help me get down from this thing? I'll owe you one if you do," I say to her as she makes it down to the bottom with ease and surveys the area. She doesn't reply to my question. She simply signals me, letting me know it's safe to come down.

"Okay, Herman, you can do this. I'm more than just some computer techie. I'm a climber? Firefighter?" I question myself, sitting down on the platform about to position myself for the climb, and suddenly, the whole platform shakes violently. I scream and grip the poor excuse of a railing as I see a man standing on the platform with me, pointing a rifle down at my head. He must have jumped in from the same window we entered.

"You're not going anywhere unless you want your head blown off. This place is off-limits to anyone other than us, so you care to explain what the fuck you're doing here?" the soldier asks. His fatigues are all black, and his face has very strong features: high cheekbones and the likes.

"This isn't what it looks like, sir. I'm here to pick up my work truck down below, but this was the only way in without causing a scene that I've gone and done anyway. Maybe you can-"

"Shut the fuck up. I have orders to shoot anything intruding on sight, so I guess your luck is up." Just then, you could hear someone trying to communicate with everyone over his radio attached to his shoulder, but you couldn't make out what he was saying from the gunfire blaring through the speaker echoing the gunfire somewhere close to the establishment.

***

I step outside this shithole of a station to take a smoke. My patience was starting to get the best of me waiting inside with Dr. Carson. I'm typically not one to smoke, but my nerves are on edge waiting for what could potentially happen. I spot one of my men walking back in from the woods after taking a leak when I see a shadow behind him emerge from the tree line. It happened so fast; I had to rub my eyes to make sure I wasn't imagining things. Then he came into focus.

"Look out behind you!"

The soldier paused mid-stride to draw his weapon as quickly as he could but not quick enough. The large man grabs him by the face and lifts him as he continues to walk towards the side of the station. I can hear a muffled scream as I drop my cigarette from my hand and grab my radio. His fully automatic weapon firing, but not at the thing carrying him. He's firing at the ground and to the sky out of sheer panic while the huge figure just keeps advancing. As they get closer, I start to recognize this face. It's the target.

"He's here! This is the captain, and the target is here at point Alpha! Everyone converge!" I shout through the radio. I look down the sights of my rifle and see him marching towards me with one of my men dying in his hand. I fire two shots at him consecutively at center mass. They connect, sending two puffs of dust flying from his chest as if my bullets hit a dirt mound. The scary part of this is that he didn't miss a step all while finally crushing the man's skull in his hand. I could see the blood burst from the top of his head right before he drops him. Just like that, a man is killed under my command. We have to take this son of a bitch down here and now. No longer concerned with what Dr. Carson wanted for the target anymore, I switch my rifle to automatic and fire at will.

*** 

Staring down at the palm of my hands, I begin to feel the power radiating through my body. It surges, giving me goosebumps as it pulses through my being. As I look around the cell, things are much vibrant, sharper even. My body feels weightless, and it's all just surreal. This is what completing the second step does to a man. These are the effects of becoming connected.

"I don't have time for your shit, asshole. Turn around and face us!" Shell commands. I turn to her, and her mouth drops open. A man in a lab coat rushes up to the cell with his eyes fixed on my face. I take a slow step towards them, and Michelle goes for her weapon, but the doctor grabs her hand, stopping her in the process.

"I'm Doctor Carson, Sean. I'm here to examine whatever it is you're experiencing. Can you tell me what you're feeling right now?" Dr. Carson isn't in the least bit frightened. His intrigue replacing what should be fear. That's when I catch my reflection in the glass window behind them. My pupils are hidden behind a white light emitting from my eyes, and my body pulses with a matching white aura.

"I feel incredible, doc," I respond in excitement. I look at Michelle and then back down at the cell door keyhole. "You have to let me out of this thing. I'm sure he knows I'm here by now, and we have to come up with a plan to take him down before he destroys us all." She looks at me, licking her lips nervously and recomposing herself to her mad dog demeanor.

"By him do you mean, Felix?" Dr. Carson asks.

I nod. It looks like someone has been doing their homework with us being the subject of study.

"We can't let you out of there just yet. There is so much more to go over with you and Felix once we capture him. I understand that Felix is a supernatural force of some kind, but I'm not sure how you fit into this equation. How are you generating all this energy around you and why is it-"

"He's here! This is the captain, and the target is here at point Alpha! Everyone converge!" We hear someone command over Michelle's shoulder-mounted radio. He's here, and I don't think they are talking about the mailman.

"We don't have time for this. Let me out of here now so we can stop this thing together," I raise my voice to them, more so towards the woman with the key. Shell shoves pass the doctor and takes off towards the door of the holding area, probably rushing off to the Alpha point. The doctor stuffs his tie back into its rightful position as a shorter man in a suit exits the watchmen's room, coming to the doctor's side.

***

The man holding me at gunpoint doesn't flinch at the command that spouted through his radio. His eyes are fixed on me through the site of his weapon, unable to miss if I make the wrong move now to challenge him. That's when Eve suddenly appears in front of me in the blink of an eye. She grabs the soldier's weapon and points it upward swiftly as it fires uncontrollably. She gives the man a swift boot, and he falls from the platform. He impacts the ground with a loud bang. Eve stands there, unharmed with the rifle in her hand, glances at the soldier below, and back at me.

"Are you okay, Herman?"

"Yeah, I'm fine. Thanks for the save, Eve. I thought he was going to shoot me. Wait. Didn't you just use your powers to get up here and save me in time? That's bad news, Eve. That Gaius thing you spoke about will probably be right on our trail now. We gotta get out here. I rather not end up in the ER today or worse. We have to go now and get Sean to safety."

"Yes, I know. However, the Gaius is already here. Sean completed another step in his training and is now able to use more cosmic energy. In doing so, he alerted Felix to our location before I did. He thinks he can take him on and win with his new power, but he is not ready. He will surely be killed, and we can't risk his death. His role in all this is much bigger than he knows. We must go," she says as she grabs me by the arm. I feel the coolness of her skin and the warmth of her touch

81

both at the same time. Before I know it, we were on the ground at the foot of the painters' platform we were standing on. She offers the rifle to me as I gawk at her.

"No thanks, Eve. I know I may look like a stone-cold killer; well, more like a serial rapist at best, but I only kill people in the cyber world. I've never actually used one of those things to kill a man before, and I don't think I ever will." She shrugs and suddenly breaks the gun into two pieces with her bare hands. Splitters of plastic and metal crumble to the floor right along with what is left of the gun. Two men appear through the door, responding to the shots fired, no doubt. More gunfire rings out as I duck away for cover.

***

Countless bullets pierce him as Felix continues his advance toward us. Reese and I are taking cover behind the hood of one of the trucks when two others are firing from the corner of the building. I stop to finally reload my rifle, and I could see a smirk on the target's face. I've witnessed a lot of things happen over my years with the Anomaly Task Force, but never have we encountered something like this. He's living proof that mankind isn't the only force to be reckoned with out here. Reese looks at me as he stops to reload, but he instead puts an M203 grenade round in the launcher below his rifle barrel. I second his plan of attack with a thumbs up, remembering that every other soldier here has a launcher available. I squeeze the button on my radio.

"Everyone at Alpha that can load up a grenade round, do so! Bullets aren't enough to stop this thing, so fire as soon as you get it loaded. Do it now!"

Reese's round fires first, hitting it in the chest and exploding on impact. We couldn't see anything except smoke and dust when the other round hit the same location and explodes. Reese reloads his rifle and drops the expended grenade round and loads another. It's then I notice that more shots were being fired from the construction area of the building – delta point. Something was happening back there, and we need to know what right now.

"Delta, what's going on back there? I need a sitrep now!" I shout over the radio while looking out, watching the dust clear from the grenade barrage at the target. It slowly clears and nothing is in the site of the impacted and singed ground. Some areas of the grass are still burning as the wind carries the smoke along.

"Looks like that got his ass, Captain Marcus. I know they want to take that thing alive, but we have to react accordingly if we want to get all these men back home to their families alive," Reese says as he turns his attention to the gunshots at Delta.

"Go check out delta while we wrap things up here, Reese. I need eyes on to know why we aren't getting any responses back and why shots are being fired back there. Go now and hurry," I command the sergeant. He nods and begins his run across the parking lot. As he leaves, I round the vehicle to take a closer look at the impact area about 250 meters out. The two men at the rear of the building do the same as we slowly make our way to the site with guns trained on the area. As we do so, I hear Reese screaming in agony. We all turn and rush to his aid, but it's too late. There were multiple sets of hands made of dirt and grass that were pulling him into the ground as he thrashes and struggles. I want to help him, but my legs are frozen still. As he sinks into the earth, Felix appears out of the ground next to him. He rises, made of mud with grass covering some of his frontal areas before finally taking human form again and appearing as he did before the explosions –unharmed and smiling.

"Your weapons cannot destroy what I am, although I do applaud your attempts," he says with humor in his voice. "Now you all must die like the pawns you are." He runs at us, full speed. The two men with me start to fire and signal me to go as they hold their ground. As I run, I look to see if Reese is still there, but he isn't. He's swallowed up by the ground itself. I rush to the entrance of the building as I can hear the men I left behind shouting and firing at the tyrant.

***

We can hear multiple shots being fired after the explosions rock the police station. Dr. Carson and his assistant stand inside, pale-faced, waiting to see what will happen next. Something in the back of my mind is beginning to tell me that Eve is here too. It's like I can feel her here. The door to the holding cell hallway burst open, and Michelle walks in with anger behind the tears in her eyes and her weapon drawn. Captain Marcus burst in right behind her.

"This is your doing. Reese is fucking dead now because of you!" she yells at me in anger. Marcus grabs her weapon and points it away from me as she fires but hits Dr. Carson in the process. He drops instantly, and the short man drops with him. Marcus is still struggling with her over the gun.

"Alright, that does it."

I grab the door to the cell and pull as hard as I could, ripping it away from the rest of the cell, sending me falling backward with the cell door in my hands. I fall on my back but feel no impact as I toss the bars next to me as if they were made of tin. I rise to my feet to see everyone staring at me in shock, except for Michelle. She aims her weapon at me, preparing to fire. Before she does, I'm across the room and out the cell, snatching the weapon out of her hand and shoving her down the hall with more force than I intend. I watch her hit the wall and crash to the floor. She sits up on all fours and shakes her head, trying to shake away the pain.

"Whoa," I say with an exhale. "I don't usually hit women, but I don't see gender when someone is pointing a gun at me."

The captain takes a swing at me. My reflexes kick in and I dodge it, instinctively. He continues to advance at me with kicks and punches. He would have been quite a match for the normal me. However, the new me can see his every step and move before he does it. His attacks are just too slow, allowing me to see every subtle move leading into his next strike. I dodge, block, and parry all his attacks as we make our way back into the cell, I was just in. Out the corner of my eye, I could see Michelle rushing to his aid. Maybe with her in the mix, they'll be able to touch me at least. Despite everything going on around me, I have to say that I'm having more fun than I should be.

# 19.

Eve just took three guys apart like they were nothing. Three supposedly trained killers, armed and dangerous, taken out by an unassuming alien woman. This is like something out of one of the comic books I read back home, but those days will be over. Things won't be the same when I get back to my apartment, that's if Vincent and his men haven't raided it and made mince out of all my computers and collector items. I stand here, hidden behind this dozer as she breaks all their guns one by one. Just as she breaks the last one, the wall facing the front of the building burst open like a wrecking ball hit it. Dust and soot pour into the room as I rush around the equipment and pallets of plywood to see what could have caused it. There he stands, the very same man that flipped a truck like he was turning a page in a book. It's Felix, and his eyes were fixed on Eve who was a few feet in front of him, but I couldn't see her reaction to his arrival.

"I've been looking all over for you, intruder," Felix utters with a satisfying smile. "You cannot be here for several reasons. Reasons that I'm sure you are aware of but choose to ignore. You know the power you use now will throw the balance of mediocrity in the garbage. What these people are taught and accustom to believing will cease to exist if you continue forward to do what you wish. I will not let you bring your wicked ways from the other plain. You have come far enough, and I cannot allow you to poison what this world has built. I must handle the situation accordingly. Exile is no longer an option for your kind. You all can't resist the urge to be here in a place where you can be a god amongst men, so you come back, back to this planet, and back to your doom by the hands of me. Your only options are a peaceful elimination or dying horribly." Eve doesn't respond right away, giving me the time I need to run back around to my original hiding spot to see her. She has determination in her eyes – determination to survive this somehow. She takes a few steps back before looking around, surveying the building, probably planning her next move.

"You don't have to do this, Gaius. I've only come here to make life better. You have your hands full trying to babysit this planet, and I want to make things easier for everyone, you included. With me here to help mankind find what their true purpose is and you guarding the atmosphere, we can do so much together. People will begin seeing that war and mayhem are unnecessary. Maybe even start to love one another," Eve pleads.

"I've watched over Earth for some time now, and I haven't needed any ascendant before you nor do I need it now. The law of the land states that none of you can come back here. Your very existence is a blight on the world. There are no Gods among men, and I'm here to make sure that this never happens, so I ask again. Will you be eliminated peacefully or die horribly? Either way, you will not leave this place." Felix's voice echoes through the emptiness of the large unfinished complex.

Eve says nothing in response as her body begins to glow softly. The air around her waves as if gas fumes were emitting from where she stands, and an eye opens in the center of her forehead. Her body is consumed fully by light. I can't make out her facial features anymore as she is now a silhouette of her former self. It is as if her skin is now made of nothing, except light. This must be her true form.

"Have it your way, intruder," Felix growls as he begins to move towards her. I could hear his footsteps stomp the pavement as he approaches, shaking the ground gently. She backs up far enough to get clear of the three unconscious men that were at her feet. He steps faster, punching directly at her as he does, but she vanishes. Just as fast as she does, she appears behind him, but he turns swiftly and backhands her. The impact of the hit sends her sprawling into a stack of plywood and 2x4s. Everything falls over violently, but she vanishes again as soon as they do. This time she appears next to him and delivers the same punch she gave one of those armed men from earlier. Felix's head snaps back, but he manages to grab her hand, forcefully yanking her towards him and delivering a head-butt to her face. She screams out in pain as he punches her in the chest. Eve flies through the air, slides along the floor, but this time she stays there. I can't let her take on this thing alone. I have to do something, or this could be the end of her right here and now. I glance at the dozer and see the key is still in the ignition.

***

The two angered soldiers attack me with nothing held back as if it was truly my fault for the death of their partner when they were the ones who took me into custody and told me to lure Felix here. They punch and kick at me with all fury. Somehow, I can feel their emotion unlike any other time before, but that isn't going to stop me from getting out of here. Dodging Marcus's kick, I push him towards the rear wall of the cell just long enough to grab Michelle by her wrist. She stares at me with fire behind her eyes, and I can feel her adrenaline pumping through her veins while she's in my grasp.

"You two aren't half bad," I say mockingly. "If this were two days or so ago, you two would have probably taken me down, but as you can see, I'm not the same ole me anymore, and you're both wasting your time and energy when we need to be after Felix. He will be in here any second now and you both should..." I stop my pleading as I hear Marcus rushing up behind me. I turn as quickly as I can, throwing Michelle at him to catch, and they both drop to the floor unexpectedly. I turn around and look at Dr. Carson and his assistant. The doctor has been shot by Michelle in her frenzy to kill me, but his wound doesn't seem fatal. The shot passed through his arm, below his shoulder. Blood is all over both of their tailored suits – maybe not tailored but expensive.

"What's your name?" I speak to the assistant from behind the bars while waiting on my two opponents to recover to decide about us against Felix.

"Samuel," he responds as the doctor opens his eyes and fixes them on me.

"Incredible, Samuel," he said without skipping a beat. "We need him to examine and find out how he's able to generate this kind of power and why. Captain Marcus, we can overlook the fact that your colleague shot me, but you have to get him back to our labs for testing and questioning," Dr. Carson commands him. My frown is aimed at the doctor.

"You're all wasting time here. The real enemy is out there. Samuel, you need to get him to a hospital before he bleeds out, and you two should just go tend to any of the soldiers that are hurt. If you're not going to help me stop Felix, then I'll just have to do it alone." My two attackers did not heed my advice, and they were back at me again. I could suddenly feel a deep feeling of fear strike from the back of my thoughts, and I immediately saw the image of Eve's battered face and felt her pain for a mere second. Felix has already got to her in the next building over, and at this rate, he'll finish her off. I've had enough of fighting these two pushovers. I dodge their attacks and strike them each with one blow. An open palm to the side of the face sent Marcus's body in a full twirl twice before hitting the ground. I knee Michelle in the stomach, and she doubles over, arms wrapped around her mid-section. I grab her forehead and shove it, causing her to trip over her partner and flop back on to the floor.

"I don't have time to play these games with you anymore. I have to save her before it's too late," I say as I make my way out of the holding cell area. I can hear Dr. Carson telling Sam to forget about him and his shoulder and follow me.

***

"Herman, don't get involved," Eve yells as she wipes the blood from her mouth while down on one knee in front of Felix. "Get out of here, quickly." Felix didn't pay any attention to me until the dozer and I were right next to him. I had the element of surprise until she shouted, although it may not have changed the outcome of the situation. The Gaius turns around and grips the top of the dozer's plow with both hands. I hammer the gas down as hard as I could while making sure I was in the highest gear I could go in. With pure strength, he pushes against the machine to keep it from running him over, and to my surprise, it's working. We are at a standstill as I continue the attempt to plow him over.

"You're the one that has a life to save here, Eve. You have to get out of here while I keep him busy. We have to complete your quest!" I say as she glares at me, knowing my decision is a brave one, but idiotic. She doesn't respond but begins to recover as I hammer on the gas of the machinery, but it's no good. I can feel it starting to give way to the powerhouse. His muscles flaring and flexing as he begins to take a slow step, pushing the dozer backward with me sitting in it. I never knew this kind of power was out in the universe and this close to home. Felix grunts loudly as his level of power seems to increase. He removes one of his hands from the top of the dozer's metal plow and places it towards the bottom. I can feel the equipment begin to lift. He lifts the front of the dozer with me tilting back in the seat, giving me no other choice but to dive out of it, hitting the pavement on my arms and knees. The impact sparks intense pain, and I look back at him. Without me holding the pedal down to repel him, he's able to do what he wants with the thing. He tilts the whole thing over my way where I landed, and I see the laws of gravity begin to take its course as he shoves it over in my direction.

"Fuck, Fuck, Fuck."

My reflexes kick in, making me roll over just in time to watch it crash down on the concrete, creating the thunderous sound of metal against freshly paved cement. The maneuver leaves me closer to Felix than I ever want to be. He kicks in a punting motion, connecting with my midsection. I feel instant pain and wind while looking at the distances between us grow further and further. I'm soaring through the air, and all I can think of is how human beings aren't supposed to fly and how terrible the landing part is going to be for me. Impacting the ground knocks the wind out of me. Gasping for air, I roll around with my hands over my ribs, hoping none of them are broken, but not being in my right mind to know if they are or not. All I can feel is pain, as the ground rumbles. I open my eyes to see Felix right above me, ready to stomp my face in. His boot begins to rise. As I look up at the sole of it, I realize that this heroic routine just isn't cut out for me. Suddenly, an instant gust of wind pulls me off the floor as his foot indents the concrete. Eve stands there with me in her arms, peering at Felix from a distance. Felix, slightly smiling, continues his assault which is now directly aimed at the both of us. Eve dodges his attacks using her vanishing ability with me in her arms along with my life in her hands. Every time she vanishes, dodging his attacks, I could see glimpses of outer space. It's almost if she is passing through outer space itself.

*** 

Bursting through the doors of the old building puts me in the makeshift hallway connecting the two of the buildings. I could hear the engine of a vehicle running in overhaul between the grunts of Felix as he attacks. Running faster than I ever ran before, I burst through the second set of doors. I see Eve and Herman rolling across the floor.

The aftermath of one of his strikes connecting, no doubt. Herman looks unconscious, and she looks exhausted and beaten. Herman is on his back while Eve's back is on top of his chest with both hands out in front of her – an attempt to protect her from the next incoming blow. As I rush to their aid, I can see Felix running towards them as if he's going to step on them at full speed. It would be as if a train ran them over.

"Eve!" I shout out as I catch his eye at the last moment before ramming into him with my forearms extended. When I connect with him, I push my arms outward, throwing him slightly off balance. He stumbles sideways, away from me. I can't allow him the time to recover, so I take the opening and attack in full force. He avoids the right hook and catches my left jab, grabbing me at the forearm with his massive hand.

"Sean, don't!" Eve screams.

I swing my free hand around, aiming at his nose and he grabs that arm too. We stand there facing one another as I struggle against his force. He's pushing my left forearm back, and I am pushing with all my might to break his grip so I can connect a punch. His face shows struggle, but not nearly as much as mine. I open my mouth and let out a battle cry as I push with what's left of my strength. He holds steady, showing no signs of faltering no matter how much force I apply. Now I can clearly see the difference between Felix and I. Eve's warnings were true. My new-found strength isn't enough to measure up to a Gaius. As the thought comes to mind, I could feel my power starting to waiver and not just because of Felix's force. All the energy it took for me to obtain this power and my actions up to this point are starting to take its toll on me. All at once, I could feel my power dissipate, and my arm hyperextends back with a snap of my elbow. All I can feel is weakness and pain resonating from my left arm. I cry out in agony as he releases the arm, and I fall to my knees. My left arm dangles by my side. My shock wouldn't allow me to continue the fight even if I had the energy. He smiles at me before his knee connects with my chin, flipping me into the air in a backflip before landing on my back.

"So, you are the one she chooses to poison in hopes of defeating me. It's a damn shame you won't be able to live to see her demise for her forbidden act of crossing the plains and coming here. I can't let you leave here alive knowing that you have obtained the knowledge from the other plain. I hate to kill a man with a family, but rules are rules, mortal. Her forbidden acts are now your own," Felix says as he approaches me. I can't tell if the ground is trembling because of his steps, or if it's just me shaking in fear of what will happen next. With blood pooling out of my mouth and searing pain coursing through me, I raise my head slightly to see this monster near me as everything around begins to go black.

"Noooo!!" Eve screams as a flash of light blares from her body before my eyes close.

# 20.

My eyes pop open, and I stare into the darkness of the room. The memories of my fight with Felix come rushing back into my mind, and I begin to wonder if this is what death looks like, but then the pain kicks in – a reminder of the living. My left arm feels like it's on fire and I don't attempt to move; not to intensify the pain. I try to sit up, but my body shudders as the ache of defeat passes through my whole being, causing me to let out a sigh of anguish and forget the notion of getting up altogether.

"You're finally awake, I see. I wasn't sure how long it would take you to recover from the ascension as well as the fight against the Gaius. Tell me, Sean, how do you feel?" Eve's voice cuts through the silence of the darkness. Her face is dimly lit somehow despite the pitch blackness in the room.

"I feel like shit, Eve. My arm is probably broken. My body is sore, and it feels like I've been working out three days without any breaks, and to top it off, I met a man that I can't fuck with."

"Sean!"

"Sean, nothing, Eve. He taught me a valuable lesson that I'll never forget. He is by far the strongest damn thing I've ever come across. I never want to see the likes of him again. I appreciate what you have done for me, but you exposed me to a whole shit load of things that I know nothing of, and I'm not sure I want to anymore. He's talked about forbidden acts and crossing plains, and I'm sure he's not talking about fucking grasslands either. "

She places her hand over my mouth to shut me up. I'm sure she wasn't happy with all the swearing, but I had so many questions to ask. Where are we? What time is it? Where did that flash of light come from and how did we manage to escape Felix when he had us in his grasp?

She brings her face over mine as she whispers, "Every second is vital from here on out. Now that you've regained your consciousness, you can begin to rest and recover properly. Let's use what's left of the night to do that. If you wish to talk to me, we can do so in your thoughts. For now, you rest." I feel like I'm falling apart, physically and mentally. I had no energy to argue with her idea of me getting rest, especially seeing how I can't get out of the spot I'm lying in now with my muscles feeling strained just to lay here. I nod at her and close my eyes.

She's there waiting for me amongst the fields of my sub-consciousness. The night sky here is full of stars, giving us light as if it was morning. The tall grass of the field unmoving. There is only stillness in the air. No sound of insects chirping. The only sound that could be heard is white noise. I could somehow make out the worried wrinkles of her face, even though her face lacks most of her solid detail. Perhaps it was just the energy I could feel radiating from her inner thoughts.

"It didn't take you long to center yourself and come back here, Sean. You've improved and grown tremendously."

"No, Eve. Enough with your pats on the head and save your "Atta boys"! You saw what that monster did to me back there even with all the enlightenment you've given me. I'm still not sure how I'm even alive right now. The last thing I remember is a flash of light, and now we're here."

"Don't be upset with yourself or me. I told you before you encountered the Gaius that you would be no match for him in your current state. You must move on to the next level if you hope to protect me from him. You must persevere."

"Protect you from him? He damn near mangled a whole army of guys back there with me included, and you still have it in your mind that I'm up for the rest of this trip? And what about the poisoning of my mind he mentioned and you breaking through some forbidden plain that you weren't supposed to?"

"We were all able to escape after I blinded him out of desperation. I wasn't even sure if flaring up my energy that way would cause such a reaction, but I'm grateful it did. It allowed us to get you and Herman to safety by moving you both into the vehicle that was parked inside. With the help of Doctor Samuel, who drove the truck, we were able to leave the area undetected by Felix. His trail on us has gone cold. Crossing the plain and his definition of poisoning is an important thing we have to discuss, and we will in due time. For now, we are safe to regenerate here in the motel so that we may complete our quest. We have less than 24 hours to get me there before it's too late."

I look up at the sky as I tread through the high grass in the field. Seeing all this is still surreal and coming this far during the quest has made me a stronger person, but what if the next encounter with Felix could be my last? I wouldn't be able to see my family anymore. My daughter grows up with some other guy pretending to be her father to get in Jasmine's pants. "I'm not sure I'm the one you need for this task anymore, Eve."

She appears in front of me and grabs me by the arms. I could feel the sadness in her grasp somehow, though she is just in spirit form. "You are the only one for this task, Sean. No one else has the power or skill to do what you can to assist me. We crossed paths because this was meant to be. You are meant to become my guardian at full strength and meant to help a wish come true. You must see this out. Your destiny is beyond this. You may not understand that now, but it is true. I know times have been difficult for you with all the changes you have undergone this past couple of days, and our chapter is ending soon, but you just have to stick with us...stick with me."

Her tone was genuine, and for once I felt as if she was more human with this level of compassion. A part of me just wants to give up on this and return to my normal life as a cable guy while the other part hears what she says. Somehow her statement resonates within me and gives me a feeling of something I haven't felt in some time: hope. "I can't promise you anything, but I did give you my word when this all began. I'll do what I can, Eve, but if Felix shows up, I can't say I'll be excited to get another bone broken like my arm or worse."

"You need not worry about your bones. Now that you reached the second level of the connection, your mind is close to centering itself. The proof around you is here as your universe begins to flourish. Your healing is accelerated more so than before. We'll rest until dawn and continue moving afterward. You should be nearly a hundred percent healed, but you must take it slow. We can't risk you not being healed at this point in our journey."

"I could have definitely used this kind of power for my old lifestyle." She frowns at me as she looks up at the sky within me. Her feet leave the ground as she hoovers upward slowly.

"Don't take your gift lightly, Sean. There is something I must prepare for you to help you later. The answers you seek when in doubt will be within when the time comes, and I must ensure that now. You are far more gifted than I am. It's just a matter of knowing what I tell you. For now, get your rest. Think about how you are going to achieve the next and final level of your connection."

I watch her fade away into the sky as I sit down. I'm not sure how I'm going to move to the next level of myself. I don't even know where to begin with no clue or hint of how to make it happen or even if I want it to happen at all. This whole situation is starting to bear down on me like a hundred-ton weight. Now that I feel alone here, I start to think about everything that's happened and why. I have to get more answers from her. She has her own agenda in all this other than saving someone's life. This person must be someone of great importance. I mean no human life is worth losing, but why is this one person, she is on a mission to save, so important to risk her life and the lives of all of us? I quiet my thoughts and lay back in the grass with my hands behind my head, gazing at the stars, pondering the possibilities.

# 21.

"The eight-ball is never your friend, Walker. Even the most precise pool player knows to fear that black beauty until you sink her in one of those elusive pockets. Of course, with her being the only thing to stop you from having to pay me twenty bones at the end of this thing, it's going to look like we were working together, but she isn't my friend. The eight-ball and I have tons of encounters like this because I'm just that damn good," Chucky says to me as he goes to line up his final shot in the dimness of the bar. I hate his cockiness and the way he speaks when describing simple things like a game of pool, but I couldn't deny that his talent on the table is a sight to marvel. "Pay attention to this shot. It's the reason why you'll be paying for the tab tonight." I shake my head with a fake grin on my face as he points the pool stick to the right corner pocket, signifying which pocket he's aiming for. I already know how this is going to end. There's no reason to keep watching, so I begin to look around to see what stragglers were left at the bar. The bar wasn't too far from where I was standing, and two older women were smoking and talking loudly, using their drunk inside voices. I could hear the door behind me open. The distinctive sound of a stick hitting the cue ball is made, and I turn my attention back to the table just in time to see the eight-ball go airborne, passing by where I was standing in the process. The sudden win means I don't have to pay him shit and the tab will be his to close. After all that shit, he was saying, he somehow fucked the shot up, and now the bragging rights are all mine along with his money.

"Looks like you're the one that needs to have deep pockets this time, Chucky. I'm not quite sure how you missed that shot, but it doesn't fucking matter now" I stop talking as I realize that whatever it is that just walked in has his attention more so than my gloating. Standing behind me with the eight-ball in hand and sunglasses is the biggest dude I've ever seen in my life. I know I'm only twenty-five and

96

I still have a lot of life to live, but I think it's safe to say that no one would be surpassing this guy's bench-pressing record at his local gym.

"Looks like we're both having an off night tonight, patron," he says as he walks over to us and throws the ball underhanded at Chucky. He catches it clumsily and nods. The man says nothing more as he makes his way over to the bar in the middle of the place. He slowly removes the shades from his squinted eyes and covers them, with the other hand briefly as if the dim lighting in here is hurting his eyes. Both Chucky and I continue to watch him as he pulls together two stool tops and sits at the bar. Across from him, you can see that the two old women have put their conversation on hold to gawk at him. The bartender for the night, Lexi, didn't acknowledge him until she noticed the silenced women.

"Bartender, I need a shot whiskey with a lime." The bass of his voice echoes across the bar, rattling glasses and shaking everyone's bones as he speaks. Lexi doesn't even skip a stride as she lays her eyes on this freak of a man. From here, it even looks like her face is in disbelief, but not because of his size. She's the owner's daughter, and she wears the crown of the princess of the palace very well. Nothing ever quite intimidates her.

"You're gonna have to throw a 'please' or 'may I' in there somewhere, big fella, if you want any service from my bar." She's the princess and all, but this guy looks like he can bring down a whole castle by himself, let alone a back-alley bar like this one. Nothing scares her, but even I'm surprised she responded to that guy like that. The room falls silent as he sits there for a few seconds.

"Please give me a double shot of whiskey with a lime," he growls. A smile comes across Lexi's face as she grabs a glass and gives him a wink.

"Don't you just want a shot of whiskey though, big guy," she teases him as she begins to pour his drink. "Not that I'm complaining. Every girl loves a whiskey-drinking man. The lime is a bit soft, but who I am to judge? You want to start a tab or are you paying cash for each drink?"

"I'm paying cash, but could you make two of those for me?" asks the big man. Lexi puts the lime on the edge of one glass and stands there with a hand on her hip with a raised eyebrow. He looks puzzled at first, but then it comes to him. "Please?" She gives another smile and grabs the other glass as requested, makes the second glass of whiskey with lime, and places them down in front of him. He pulls some money out of his back pocket and hands it to her. "Keep the change." She looks at the money, and the expression on her face brightens up like a child on Christmas Day. Must have been way more money than the princess was expecting. He downs the first drink quickly and places the glass back on the counter slowly and grabs the second one. Like magic, Chucky appears next to me, giving me the money he owes from the bet.

"Don't just stand there. That freak messed up my shot, and I demand a rematch. Get some change for the table and some more beers on the tab," he says to me while digging in his back pocket to grab his smokes. I wasn't too thrilled about having a rematch with him. His temper shows whenever he doesn't get his way, and I'm not a fighting man like he is. To avoid trouble, I comply. Besides, another beer would be right up my alley. I lay my pool stick across the table and begin to make my way to the bar. I get there and sit on the corner, far away from the huge dude just to make sure I wasn't anywhere near his personal space bubble. I watch Lexi as she leans back against the cooler, revealing her butterfly tattoo along with tribal signs to match over her belly button. Her huge, propped up titties are enough to catch any man's attention every moment she looks away, but he didn't seem to care much. He didn't even sneak a glance.

"Can I get another beer, please, Lexidoll?" I say, sliding the money across the bar. "I need some more quarters for the table as well, darling." She glances over at me briefly, then turns her eyes back to the visitor. She put her index finger up at me, telling me to give her a minute.

"So, what's your name, well-tipping stranger?" Lexi says to him with her head slightly tilted. The man took a sip of his drink and barely looked up at her as he sets the glass down, dropping the lime in the whiskey without squeezing it.

"My name is irrelevant to you but even more so to myself. If you must call me something, 'Felix' will do just fine."

"Felix works just fine for me, baby. You look like you have had one hell of a day, and a little conversation over your whiskey wouldn't hurt now would it?"

He takes the glass and looks at her through the dark liquid. "My woes are beyond anything you'll ever know. I'll save you and me the time while I drown out the flames of my defeat with this drink." He takes another sip of the whiskey.

"My dad had me around this bar long enough to know what's what around here, and I can tell you're different from the average Joe. I heard all kinds of stories around here, so I'm sure you don't have one that I ain't never come across, Felix. Just try me is what I'm saying, big fella."

He stands up from the bar and drinks the rest of his whiskey like it was water, and he sits the glass down. "I'm looking for some people. I found them, but I lost them, and the odds of me catching them again are highly unlikely. And the fate of the world depends on it. I can't let them get out and spread the toxicity of their ways to the rest of the world. Everything you know and find comfort in such as your religions, what you perceive as real, and what you think life is, will be ruined. Centuries upon centuries of teachings destroyed all because of one fallen star's selfish desires. No intruder has ever gotten past me since I took watch, and I don't plan on letting it happen now."

Lexi simply nods with a frown. Whatever this guy has going on is too complex for any of us in this small town to understand, and I hope she doesn't try to relate.

"Well, I'll be damned, Felix, you are right. That is some shit I never heard before the whole time I've been here, and I don't know what to tell ya besides to keep at it and hope for the best," she says. Then she flips a bar towel over her shoulder and walks off to the other side of the bar, probably trying to get away from him and whatever craziness he has to say next.

His green eyes pass over me and darts to Chucky. He rubs the edges of his eyes with his fingertips and says "You should take a shot of whiskey. Looks like you suffered a defeat of your own, patron when you scratched on that eight-ball. I'll leave you with something to remember. A lesson of sorts for both you and me is to be more precise, more vicious with our will the next time we get a chance. Defeat and whiskey shots are something that will happen, but never give up."

Chucky said nothing as the giant walked away from the bar and became a shadow as the door slams close.

# 22.

I could see our new-found friend, Samuel, staring at me out of the corner of my eye as I slowly bend my freshly healed arm back and forth to work the kinks out of it. I can understand his surprise. He probably saw me in pain with my arm twisted all up and broken, and now, after a night's rest, he sees me up before anyone else, fully recovered mostly. My body still has some soreness, and my arm is still stiff as if I slept on it wrong. "What's the matter, Samuel? Never seen a broken arm mended after a good night's sleep?"

The scientist shakes his head. "I've never seen anything as remarkable as you or her. Another reason why I'm happy to get a closer look at what you truly are and what your plans are for the rest of us. I do wish Dr. Carson was here because he knows a lot more about this line of work than I do. He spent all his adult life studying things and events that were centered on Universal Science. As his assistant, there were times I would think he was losing his mind. Everyone at NASA considered the branch he was placed in charge of, World Anomaly Division or WAD, a dead-end section. It appeared that way as they seem to place researchers that had come to an early end of their careers there to keep them under their watchful eyes while giving some support to veteran researchers' half-cocked ideas. Wouldn't want any of the secrets of space getting out to the public. Now with the appearance of Eve and whatever effect she has on you, I can say that Dr. Carson did not lose his touch."

"If that's the case, Sam, how did you get stuck in such a crap department at your young age? Either you excel at what you did, and they think more of the section than you do, or you pissed someone off and got the short end of the stick," I respond, finally turning to face him as he leans on the tattered dresser. He smiles slightly, remaining silent as the sound of a key being inserted in the doorknob and twisted can be heard. In walks a battered, not so healed, Herman. His face freshly bruised and scratched but with new apparel on. His khaki cargo pants still have the creases of the department store they came out of along with his blue and purple horizontal striped short sleeve button up. His hair is all over the place, and his glasses are bent and tapped on one side. He enters the room, holding bags with Eve following right behind him. Her hair is tied back in a ponytail as the light from the morning sun hits her silky pale skin. We can all see that she too is also completely healed. Wearing a new, thin, navy blue and gray long sleeve shirt and black leggings, you couldn't tell she had to fight for her life the day before in the slightest. Her sleeves are pulled up slightly above her wrists, and she looks a lot like one of those athletic soccer moms.

"Didn't mean to eavesdrop on you guys conversation, but you can blame that on these thin motel walls. How do they expect anyone to get any sleep around this place? If talking with a mild tone can be heard through the windows, so can other activities, if you get my drift? I digress. Did I hear you say something about Universal Science and World Anomaly Division, Samuel?" asks Herman with a look of interest in his eyes. "I read forums and spoke among other online chatrooms across the web about the subjects. Me being the guy I am, a computer hacking genius extraordinaire, did some digging and concluded that Universal Science is the collective study of Earth and its relationship with everything in the universe. Some of the things I found were highly interesting. Things like the other planets that have been discovered in another galaxy light years away from ours and the alien ships or entities that may or may not have been encountered to cross these distances by folding space and traveling through wormholes. However, even with my hopes of truth to some of the sci-fi space stories I know of, I considered it all mythical talk until Sean here brought the truth to me in a diner only two days ago." Herman sits down the bags and Eve sticks her hand in it and pulls out gas station breakfast sandwiches. I'm not sure what these things have in them, but I'm starving. She distributes them to us along with orange juices and bottled waters. Herman throws me a bag on the bed next to me. He points at it and nods. "Being your identity coordinator, I already know you go with the tough guy look, so I did my best to accommodate you with what they had in town. We can't have you walking around in that bloody and ripped up grunge look you got going on now, so I took care of you. You can thank me later, Sean."

"I appreciate it, Herman. Maybe you should have brought some makeup in there to cover all those battle scars you have on your face. Was that your first scuffle, little guy? My little nerd is growing up right in front of my eyes," I tease.

"I'm sorry that I don't have inherent galactic healing abilities like you and Eve, but I can just say I had an MMA fight last night." He looks around the room to check everyone's approval rating of his tale. Seeing that none of us are buying it, he continues to say, "Fine. Car accident it is. Just so you all know, you guys suck the fun out of being creative."

Sam nods with a smile and says, "To get back to the topic at hand, I agree, Herman. Everything you stated about Universal Science is correct to an extent. Just know that most of the relative studies done on the subject were completed by my mentor, Dr. Carson. His studies have concluded that we as people are connected to the universe in some type of way that goes further than evolution. We can't use the term soul or spirit because that would debunk all things scientific, yet he found that we are a part of the scheme of the universe. The idea stemmed from him originally after having some dream about our bodies being made of some otherworldly material. I sometimes think that he thinks that he had some type of space encounter in the past or something. Either way, I'm hoping to shed some light on it all with the help from you, Eve." Sam saying that reminds me of the answers Eve promised to give me earlier while we were in my subconsciousness. Seeing how I have some brainpower in the room, I can ask her freely without fear of being lost in the explanation knowing that Herman will translate.

"That's all really riveting, fellas, but I have an unanswered question myself for her," I say as Eve turns to me with her prism eyes looking through me. "What exactly did Felix mean when he said you broke the plain and poisoned my mind?" The room stands still in silence as she stares at me for a moment before looking back at everyone in the room. It wasn't until now I notice that this was a nonsmoking room, but it still carried a faint scent of old cigarette smoke. I could see her lips part, but nothing comes out as if she's searching for the right things to say or simply buying time to lie. I spent a long time lying to my family, especially to Jasmine, and I know what it looks like when you want to conceal something.

"I truly don't think now is the best time to discuss all of this, Sean. Daylight is burning, and this is the last day we have to get there to complete the task at hand."

"She makes a lot of sense there, Sean. We should leave immediately. I don't like staying in one place too long because Felix is out there ready to kill us on sight," Herman says as he takes a bite of his breakfast sandwich. "We have to get going and get this done before it's too late or all of these bruises on my handsome face would be for nothing."

I shake my head, "I'm not going anywhere until I get an understanding of what we are truly doing here and why does it have to be so important? I know saving a life is one thing, but after being called poisoned, I'm more curious about what this whole thing means." I glare at Herman and Eve, catching a glimpse of Samuel. His eyes are narrowed as he waits to hear her response. I hate to put her on the spot like this, but this has gone on long enough without me asking for answers, especially after almost dying for her. "I damn near died back there, and I want to know why this one life is so important. Why is this Gaius chasing us down and willing to kill all of us for associating with you? And why does he want to kill me for having the powers you help me discover?"

Eve sighs. She steps away from us and paces up and down the living room area of the motel. Looking at the other two in the room shows that at least Herman and I were lost. Sam still has a look on his face as if he forgot to turn off the flux capacitor before leaving his home to encounter a celestial being today. He looks as if he's calculating something of his own. She finally stops pacing and faces us with a hand on her hip. This is the most human I've ever seen her look. She takes in a big breath of air and exhales slowly.

"Sean, you do deserve the truth about everything, and I'm sorry I wasn't fully honest with you when this first began. Just know I wasn't hiding the truth for my benefit, but because this outcome will help us all in the long run whether you got the complete story about the plains or not."

What do you know? Even women from outer space have a lying streak in them.

# 23.

Eve's concern can be seen by all of us. I had tugged at a door she is not ready to open, and maybe she never was planning to open it. She sits down next to the old school television on the dresser and fixes her eyes on me. I can tell how she feels about having to share this information. As my connection matures within, so does our own. She is going through something in her mind that I can't quite grasp. Maybe after she spills the beans, I'll be able to pinpoint what I see behind those starlit eyes.

"I know I held the illusion that I'm not of this world, and from the way we met, Sean, you had every right to assume so, but the reality is that I'm more like you all than you think. I used to be a woman bound to herself and everything around her such as family, friends, and even possessions until one day I stumbled across a new way of life. A life we all were meant to live, one without fear or worry or even death. It all came to me in a vision one day while living a normal life. Since that day, I was determined to make life the way I know of it now. I studied everything for months about our relationship with the great beyond. I studied and meditated so much that I found the way to see within myself."

"What you're saying here is that you were once human and somehow you managed to dive within your subconsciousness like you trained me to do when we first met?" I ask, not believing she could do such a thing without some sort of guidance. Herman waves his hand at me and places a finger over his lips. He's telling me to shut up. I think about punching him in the chest, but he's right. She muscled up the bravery to share whatever story she has to share with us, and I should hold my questions to the end before I make her lose her nerve.

"Yes, Sean. I did exactly what I've been training you to do yourself these past two days, but the difference is I had no guidance. My

105

studying on the matter persisted for months until I found the path. Once my eyes were opened, I worked night and day to become what I have guided you to do. When I touched your mind back in your apartment, I bestowed upon you the belief of what we can become. The relief of knowing that there is something more to life was the ecstasy you felt." Her eyes still set on me without blinking. "I managed to overcome all things and connected after a week. The connection opens your psyche to everything in the universe. All the knowledge and questions that were left unanswered by the mortality of those before us were all there to see, but only as I meditated. Once the meditation was over, I couldn't remember any of the answers. I was able to acknowledge I had traveled to the other plain; however, my human mind was not able to retain the vast knowledge it had to offer me. Only as I traveled the unknown did I see all the answers. The answers to questions about gods, pyramids, and even how the cosmos came to be. I wanted those answers for myself, so I dared to travel further each time to discover a way to expand my physical mind to do so. One day, I ventured too deep into the stars, and I couldn't find my way back. I was lost in the other plain with no way to return to my human counterpart. It's virtually impossible to find your way back if you travel too far for answers, so I came up with another plan. That's when I fell to Earth, breaking the plain by binding myself to a star. This star is like no star that our world has known. No telescope can see them because they exist far above our solar system, even far above what houses our solar system. This star is made in the other plain for us to connect to and be what we are meant to be in this world; people without worry or envy."

Glancing over at Samuel, I can see that he was sweating with questions and the anticipation of asking them. His face wrinkles up as if she said something that hurt his feelings, and without waiting for the story to be at the end, he says, "So you found a way to bind yourself with a planet of some kind? I understand you were an entity in another dimension so to speak, but how do you even begin to do such a thing? Describe how this action takes place and all the science it takes to do such a task."

Eve shakes her head. "You see, you all rely on your science to define what cannot be defined in such a way. All the stars you see in the sky aren't all planets and suns. A lot of them are what your studies have said for them to be, but in the reality of things, the stars are a projection of your inner self trying to show you everyone's connection to the universe. Everyone's potential can connect to their star. The star is a physical representation of your inner self manifested, but it also a gateway to the other plain. You have to find yourself out there before you can become one with it as I have and come home to Earth."

"Wait a minute, Eve," Herman interrupts to make sense of things. "What this means is that your soul connected to the star which acted as some kind of portal. That's why you came from outer space. You had to travel from there to reach Earth. Not because you jumped out the backdoor of some UFO, but because you were trying to get back to this plain. I know it's crazy, but it all makes sense to me somehow." Eve nods with a look of amazement across her face before a slight smile appears. Herman's brain reminds me of a box full of hamsters; constantly moving about itself with no rhyme or reason. He's able to understand the most complex scenarios. I peek at the scientist, and he's just starring down at the brown-stained carpet of the motel, his mind trying scientifically to make her words mean something in the ways of his subject matter; to the textbook ways of a scientist. But I still have some questions of my own.

"What you're saying doesn't add up to me, Eve, or whatever, whoever you truly are. I found you in the most unlikely place saying things like this is my destiny or how my definition of time was much different than your own. Not to mention the whole reason we've made it this far to begin with which is because-"

"What of the life you wish to save, Eve?" Herman interrupts. "What does reaching that hospital to save that life have to do with you?" She turns to the mirror and looks into her own eyes, searching for the words to say yet again. I can see the same look in her eyes from earlier; one that shows turmoil underneath the all-powerful woman she is.

"It is a task I must complete to stay here in order to help Sean and others like him that are lost. That person is very important to my connection and the true reason I had to break the plain. Believe it or not, the childhood tale of wishing upon a star is truer in my case than you may ever know. As far as the matter of time goes for me, things are different. Traveling from where I was in the physical universe, after breaking the plain, allowed me to go back through time to catch up to this date. While traveling, I knew I couldn't do this alone. The answers were all laid out for me once I became connected. I could see the outcome of what would happen to me without the help of another and showed a journey ending in death with no one knowing how to obtain their true self. That's when you, Sean, started to come into view. Once I landed, I knew you were going to be there to help me somehow, and the only answer I have for that is simply fate. Our paths were meant to cross, and because you were there to help me without knowing anything about me or of me, everything about you and who you can be reached out to me." She exhales and continues, "Once we met, I wasn't sure how to convince you to walk this path with me. I tried dangling fate in your face, but you weren't obliged to react to that. However, when I offered a chance to get power beyond your wildest dreams, you happily walked the line with me."

"That wasn't my deciding factor, but it did help. You told me all this would help me get my family back, but it sounds like you said all that philosophical bullshit just to use me. You used me because I had a history of fighting, and that's the kind of backup you need when it comes to fighting a Gaius. Well, you see where that fucking got us, right? You used me from the get-go," I respond in anger.

"Don't think of it that way. Think of it as we both get what we desire. I get to remain here once this is all over, and you get to have endless power, a profound view of self-worth, and the means to get your family back with all the clarity you found within. I didn't use you or force you to do anything that you didn't agree to do."

"No. You just baited me into it instead. You knew I wouldn't be able to resist that deal. Fuck, who could?"

"Enough of the swearing, Sean. I only wanted to share the truth as you asked so we can be on our way now. We have to leave and cover as much ground as we can before it's too late for me, for us."

"Too late for you?" I say with a flare of anger in my voice. "Tell me star woman person. What exactly happens to you or us if you don't get to save this life?"

"The same thing that happens to any star that has reached its life expectancy; I become a supernova."

I look at Herman who is standing there with his mouth open while Samuel casually clears his throat to speak.

"And what kind of explosive force are we talking about, Eve?"

"A devastating one."

Herman jumps in place with excitement. "I get it now. The life you want to save is so important to you because that life isn't just some random person. It's the next person you plan to share your enlightenment with!"

# 24.

After I let Eve's information settle into my mind, I jumped in the shower to help think things over while the others were still waiting on me. The shower is my very own getaway for fifteen minutes or so. There's something about the hum of a showerhead and the heat of the water that helps me see things clearer. In here, I begin to think about all the events that have happened that led me to this point in my life. Meeting Eve has been quite a problem for me. She should've come at a more convenient time for me like when I was facing all my childhood and teenage problems as a juvenile delinquent. Who am I kidding? I would've told her to shove it and probably tried to kick her ass or take the power and do some real damage to all those people I fought in the past. With this kind of power back then, I wouldn't have to hide from my former identity. I could be me. Maybe I would have realized a lot sooner than being with my family meant more to me than bashing in rival gang members and people that owed my boss money at the time. I can't think of those days without Jasmine rushing back to give my memory a slap, promptly. Recalling my time in the jail cell yesterday meant seeing her and my daughter with another man, happy and playing blissfully in the kitchen in a house I paid for out of the guilt I carried for my past antics. I wonder if they've seen all the incredible things happening right now. If they know that I'm more than some dad who abandons his daughter for personal gain, although that was the motive at the time.

Now that the truth has been revealed by Eve, I'm not sure I have it in me to continue anymore. We're only a few hours out from the hospital, and if she keeps her power off the radar, she can achieve her goal without getting torn apart by Felix. Enough of this pretending to be a hero. I have to get back to my normal life of cabling houses for television and weekend visits to catch a glimpse of Jasmine with all her perfection which I loved so much and spend time with Jada. I hated

110

that I took all that time for granted when I told her I would never do such things again. I dry myself off and throw on a pair of jeans and a gray t-shirt with the words "North Carolina" in blue with a star below it, faded by design. Clothes brought by Herman and picked out by Eve from some gas station clothing hole in the wall. Ironic that they chose this shirt. When I get out of the bathroom, Eve was staring out the window while Sam and Herman were writing down something as they sat across from each other. I'm sure they're trying to crack some kind of science code comparing this situation and the meaning of life. I'm still trying to grasp the concept of Eve being special, yet not so special. That at some point, she was like me. Aside from running from the mob and fighting to see my family, she was human. Maybe she had a family. A husband that worked all the time while her children ran her wild. That would be enough reason to find a new meaning to life. She turns to me as if she can feel me studying her.

"We must leave now so we can make the deadline in time. I have no intention of self-destruction. I set out on this to change lives and save others. We must continue," she says, looking at all of us with determination in her glare.

"We can leave right after I call my family," I say. My guilt of forfeiting my time with Jada for my selfish gain has put me back in the shoes of a younger me. Going around, doing as I please for my own selfish interest while tearing the heart of my wife apart. "I have to let them know I'm okay." I turn to the door and begin to walk as I mutter to correct myself. "I have to know if they're okay."

Herm and the doctor simply nod and go back to working as Eve begins to shove some clothing items and things into a bag. She is starting to get impatient with us, but she has no other choice. Only to take us with her. I haven't gotten to the bottom of why just yet, but just like the rest of what happened in the past couple of days, there is a reason for it. Walking along the sidewalk of the motel, I could see a payphone in front of the lobby. I haven't used one of those since I was a teenager while waiting to receive orders from my boss all those years ago. I get to the phone and dial the only number I remember off the top of my head: Jasmine's. The phone takes a moment to connect me to her, and I glance through the lobby windows – which needed some cleaning – to see the time on a digital clock above the check-in counter. It's a little past noon. The phone rings longer than usual before it finally stops mid-ring, telling me that someone has finally picked up the phone.

"Jazzy, I'm happy you picked up. It's me, Sean. Now before you hang up on me, I want you to know tha-"

"Let me stop you right there, lover boy." A male voice cuts me off. "My woman is tending to my soon to be stepdaughter at the moment. I would take a message for her, but given you put this bruise on my face a couple of days ago, forgive me if I don't give a shit."

It's Kevin. My blackout beating must have left him bitter. The new me would have turned the other cheek, maybe even apologized, but I'm not feeling motivated to be that me anymore, especially when he thinks he is safe from me. "Maybe you didn't learn from the ass kicking I gave you before, but I'll be happy to clear the lesson up for you next time we meet, Kevin."

He scoffs at my response. His bravery is at an all-time high, knowing that I'm not close enough to wring his neck. "I do not doubt that you would be happy to teach me a lesson, but I've done some learning of my own. Learning about who you really are, Hammer."

I take the phone away from my ear and fire a sharp glare at it as if I could see Kevin through it, wishing he could feel the heat radiating from my being to get my hands on him for mentioning my old name. "What does that matter? You should know if you've done any research on me that I'm not the man you want to fuck with in any situation.

"Yes. I must admit, at first it did shake my resolve a bit learning of your past life until I started to dig a little deeper. I went deep with some ties I have all around the state to find out you pissed off some very bad people. People that I don't normally associate myself with, but for you, I made an exception. Does the name Vikor Capala ring any alarms for you, dickhead?"

My heart sank. I know Jasmine hates me, but I don't see her giving away my past life information to this guy. She hasn't betrayed me or put me behind bars all these years, and I don't believe she ever will.

"Judging by your silence, I'm going to assume that's a yes. Well, I had my people talk to his people, and we came up with a brilliant plan. Viktor and I do not have a whole lot in common. He likes action films while I'm a horror kind of guy. He likes Sinatra, and I prefer Al Green.

He likes being a successful crime boss while I like being a successful businessman. We did seem to find some common ground when it came to revenge though. We both hate you and want you gone. Once we found that out, we were able to cut a deal. One where we both get what we want."

My anger subsided only to the fear of what happens if I don't give them what they want. This man is with my family, has access to them at any time of the day. Does Viktor know this already? I take the phone and place the upper receiver against my forehead. No matter how far I run or how much I regret the past, it always seems to catch up with me in one shape or form of karma or another. "What do you want?" I ask through gritted teeth.

"Simply give me your location. Viktor and company have been eying the news and following the strangeness you've been leaving behind as you travel. You tell me where you are, and you won't have to worry about him coming here to visit Jasmine or Jada and using them as leverage to get you because you're a coward.

"I've never been a coward, and I'm not going to start now, but you're bluffing. I know you care for them almost as much as I do. You wouldn't have their blood on your hands and take the consequences of me having your blood on my hands afterward."

"That's where you're wrong, Hammer," Kevin snarls. "From the second you laid hands on me the other day, I've been thinking of a way to return the favor of you taking my pride away from me. We all know a man's pride can supersede love any day of the week. I thought that getting your family to be mine was enough, but my thirst was not quenched. That's when I decided to see if I can hurt you more and here's my opportunity. I always get what I want, and I always win. Next time you should know who you are going up against before you strike someone and put yourself in a situation you can't get out of."

My hands are tied. I can't risk Viktor going after my family. Looks like my anger has gotten the best of me as Eve tried to stir me away from early in the weekend. I have no choice if I want my family to stay safe. Even if he was bluffing, I have no way of telling. My options are limited. There is only one way out. The choice to stay or go with Eve has been decided for me. From here we go our separate ways.

# 25.

"We're leaving the motel right now and heading to some hospital a couple of hours away from here. There is so much I want to explain to you now, but my time is limited because we're leaving," I say to Dr. Carson from my cell phone. "The things I saw and heard while accompanying them so far confirms some of your theories while completely throwing others out of the equation."

"Excellent work, Samuel," the doctor says with excitement in his voice. He is dying to know what I know, but he knows I can't be in the lobby here for long or they could leave me. "I won't hold you up. Keep me updated on what happens throughout your trip. I know all this was sudden for you, being with them like this, but be brave. All scientists have to explore the unknown to get the answers they seek. Those before you have done it and I have done it. It's the cost of getting the answers that need to be written into the history books."

I don't doubt anything he says now. His curiosity of it all gave him the bravery to approach Felix during our first encounter with him. The very same Felix that decimated an elite force of men and women of the World Anomaly Task Force, almost single-handedly, and could have easily torn us apart during that initial encounter. "I understand, Dr. Carson. How are your wounds and how are our NASA overseers taking all this? They can no longer turn a blind eye to your work after such an incident." They were never too fond of the doctor's hypotheses, and when I was forced into the job of working with him, I must admit, it wasn't my first choice of positions in the government industry.

"They do believe my studies now, yes, and they are undergoing an extensive investigation at the 'Sunflare.' That's what they are calling the police station where the events took place. You need not concern yourself with that right now, Samuel. The work is no longer just my work; it is yours's now as well. Just keep traveling along with them, learning what you can and update me as often as you can via text. Gathering another team in an attempt to capture any of them is going to cause more casualties. Instead, I'll come to meet you so we can discuss all this and add myself to your party once you let me know about your destination."

"Thank you. I'll do just that. Talk to you again soon." I hang up the phone and turn in the room keys to the man behind the counter. He's an old man with white hair escaping from the center of his head and hanging from the ledges of his temples all around the length of his skull. He barely looks up at me as he mumbles our room number. I could smell the liquor on his breath. The frail man says nothing more and returns his attention to the magazine. Opening the door, I could see Eve reluctant to leave Sean with one foot in the vehicle and another out as she watches the building we were staying in, expecting him to burst out of the room any minute. Somehow, I know he wouldn't. Herman jumps out of the driver seat and makes his way around to the passenger seat, shooting a quick look at the building and then Eve.

"Should we try to bring him along again, Herman?" I ask, making my way to the driver seat from the porch of the lobby. Herman looks up towards the clear sky as if he's pondering on the subject. His head suddenly snaps back towards me.

"No. None of us are capable of dragging him out of there without risking life and limb. Another thing to keep in mind here is that a whole group of killers, dealers, and wheelers are headed here to probably do just what their names suggest, and I know they want both, Sean and myself, dead. Probably you two as well because you're guilty by association, and then there's the walking, talking, cosmic time bomb in our back seat here that needs to be somewhere to defuse itself. Now, taking all that into consideration here, Samuel, I vote to let him be. Now get in the truck if you're going."

Eve expression turns into a slight smile as she closes the door and looks at me, amused at Herman's deductive reasoning skills. I simply exhale and jump into the driver seat, shift the gear into drive, and begin our trip.

***

I wish things could have been different for my family. Maybe if my past wasn't such a train wreck, I would have had a better chance of being a decent father and husband. Instead, I chose money, power, and respect over anything that is supposed to be important to me. I spent my years surrounded by violence. I grew up being a victim, then dishing it out as a teen and adult, thinking that it was the only way I could survive in the world. When Jada was born, it was supposed to be the end of that lifestyle. The life that kept me and anyone I cared about in danger, hence the new identity. Things were starting to pan out decently for a while, then all this happens. Some sort of spiritual star girl plummets down into my world and changes it all. The sins of my past follow me still, and here I am, back in a life of violence, with my family in danger because I'm too stupid to control my anger and unable to escape what's likely to become of me. I turn off the TV and finish my bottled water. The water was a little above room temperature as I gulp it down. My nerves are starting to show as I look at my hand tremble while holding the empty plastic bottle, but that was the least of my concerns at this point. Even with all the power I acquired, I'm still nervous about what Viktor and his animals are going to do to me once they arrive.

"Maybe it's best things come to this. My family won't be in this situation again. I wouldn't have to worry about being anyone's protector or getting the shit kicked out of me by some musclebound planetary freak." I shrug and place the bottle down on the dresser. I could hear cars pulling up to the motel. I pick up the phone and call the front desk.

"Front desk," the man says with annoyance in his tone, not trying to hide his drunken slur.

"Hey, listen. There may be some yells and shouts coming from my room, but it's just me playing around with some old friends of mine, so no need to call the police or anything. If we get too loud down here, just give us a call. Just thought I'd get a jump on any complaints you might get before we reunite," I say.

"We don't have anyone in the rooms around you, buddy. Things should be fine. I'll give you a call otherwise." The phone clicks and dial tone is all I hear. He's the pinnacle of customer service.

I look out the window and see two sedans outside. All the men step out of their cars. Seven men appear wearing slacks and polos. Their eyes covered by dark designer sunglasses, making their face seem colder, more emotionless. The passenger door opens from the second sedan, and there he was, Viktor Capala, here in the flesh to finish the job himself. I clear my throat and open the door. He looks at me and snatches the shades off his face, looking around the area carefully before whispering something to the man next to him and smiling at me.

"Can't say I'm happy to see you, Viktor, but I don't think anyone ever is. That's a face only a mother could love."

"Always so witty, screwdriver," he responds. "I've always hated all your jokes and taunts, but I have my own joke now, and I'm sure you'll get the punchline."

"My name was never screwdriver, Viktor," I respond, attempting to talk away the butterflies. "Maybe you have me confused with one of those guys your mom had coming in and out of her bedroom when you were a kid. What did she tell you? This is Santa's helper making sure that you're a good boy this year?"

Viktor scuffs, glancing at another man and nudges his head in my direction. The muscle rushes over and delivers a blow to my stomach, shoving me inside the room.

"Why aren't you laughing now, saltshaker?" Viktor gloats in amusement.

# 26.

I've been here before: hands handcuffed behind my back as I wiggle in discomfort against the wooden chair, blood running down my battered and bruised face, and pain bouncing from both sides of my face from blows dealt by a hail of punches and slaps. His brother had me like this before years ago, but I somehow made it out alive. Back then I had a whole crew of people that were willing to help me, willing to die for me. I left those people and that life behind, yet the same situations have not left me. Viktor and his men sit all around my motel room, taking turns bashing me. They didn't have much to say before the attack begun. Now that they got some aggression out, they're all taking a smoke break.

"Looks like you've seen better days, monkey wrench," Viktor chuckles. "You thought I would let you and Sebastian go after the pain and suffering you caused my family? The dishonor you did my brother by killing him in his home?" He pauses, waiting for me to respond but I'm still reeling from the pain of it all. "You're not as talkative as your boss was, old friend. He had much to say before, during, and after his beating. Unfortunately, he didn't have a lot of his simple motor functions to talk by the end of our session with him, and we had to put him down. He's the one that told me about your so-called new life mere hours away from your old life. I'm appreciative of you and your stupidity. I would have gone much further away if I was running from a man of my caliber." Viktor stops and rubs the red on his knuckles before his expression changes. He suddenly looks disgusted.

"Perhaps you thought ill of me, dustpan. You thought of me like some little shit who wouldn't be capable of finding you, not even if you were right under my nose, yes? Was that it?"

I lift my head and give him a bloody grin and a shrug. Viktor strikes me almost instantaneously.

"You will pay for your disrespect. I'm going to give you the most pain possible today before I kill you." The Russian unbuttons his shirt and rolls up the sleeves of his silk shirt further. I close my eyes and rest while I still can. Suddenly, I'm back within myself, standing in my inner field, but it's different. The sky is a deep red hue with dark black clouds lingering about. Some spots of the field of grass are dead while other parts don't have grass at all. Looks as if the land is barren just as it was before I completed the steps. My connection must be fading out. That explains why I'm in so much pain.

"What do you think you're doing, Sean?" Eve says as she walks up behind me. I don't turn to acknowledge her transparent form. I could still feel the disappointment in her voice striking me down to my core. "Judging by the appearance of your world, you are starting to revert into where you were before. You have mastered and come so far within yourself, and you're just going to let all you've gained go? It doesn't make sense to do this, Sean. You must reconsider and persist."

"I can't let anything happen to them, Eve. You may not quite understand because everything you seem to do up until this point was all a lie. You make your cause sound so great, but ultimately, you just want to gain more for yourself. Everything you've shown me and told me is more to benefit you than me."

She rushes her steps to see the look on my face before she says anything. "I know I wasn't a hundred percent honest with you when we first met. You may have even felt like a tool with the deal I gave you, but you must understand, this isn't just about me, and it never has been, Sean. A life hangs in the balance. Just think, if that life belonged to any of your family members, you would do anything to stop that from happening, correct?"

"Yes, Eve. That's why I'm here to end this problem that's going to chase my family and me until I'm dead. Being here and coming this far with you in this whole connection thing has shown me that my past has done nothing more than sculpt out a life full of suffering for those around me. I'm tired of running from it and stressing about it. I've completely lost my family, and the only way I can help them now is by sacrifice."

Her face glows faintly as she flashes a quick smile. "I'm happy you realize that coming out of all this will take sacrifice. You don't have to die to end this, Sean, you self-defeating man. Things are bad right now, yes, but you can conquer this. You've grown so quickly since we met and that's not just because of me alone. You willed it to be. Take this newly found power and do what I'm attempting to do. Save a life and make a family happy again. You can do just that, Sean. Save your life and make your family happy. They've experienced you at your worst. You owe them the best part of you. Give them the universe, Sean."

Her words resonate within me. She knows what kind of outcome I want. I don't know if it's because she knows me or because she has access to my thoughts and can easily map out what I require out of life, but either way, she's right. I just want to see the smiles on Jasmine and Jada faces', and those smiles will be there because of me. Deep down, my family does love me. If I die now, I'll never be able to give Jada the life I wasn't able to live. Not to mention the fact that Jasmine would never forgive me. I can't die here today, but I must settle things with Viktor once and for all and then handle that snitch, Robert. "Alright, Eve, you convinced me. I'll continue to fight for them as I started to when Jada was born. The goal is to take care of my family, and I can't do that if I'm dead."

"That's more like it, Sean. When you're done here, you'll have to catch up to us. I have a feeling that the Gaius will be making an appearance soon, and you're the only one that can defeat him."

I cringe to the thought of facing Felix. "Hold on, Star lady. Let's not get ahead of ourselves here and take this thing one step at a time," I quip. She smiles and begins to walk away. "Before you leave, I want you to know that once all this over, I'm going to have a list of personal questions to ask you if we make it out of this, like your real name and where you grew up and all that. You haven't gotten off the hook yet, Eve.

She smiles while she slowly vanishes away.

I turn my attention to the field, beginning to focus. I remember the overcoming of my past with my father and letting go of my family due to my selfishness. My body remembers the sensations of coming through the steps and starts to tingle. Heavy rain begins to fall as the black clouds dissipate. The grass begins to grow in the dirt spots, and bright greens begin to return to the layout of it all. The rain was my will, floating away from my consciousness, captured in those black clouds. Life returns to the field as the sky is now as blue as ever all around except on the horizon. It's still dark as night, but I feel reassured because it's the way it's meant to be. I fall back into the lush, wet grass with a smile. The rain stops. I feel my strength slowly returning. I shut my eyes for a second and open them.

Here I am, back in reality. My hands handcuffed behind my back, blood, and sweat pouring down my face, full of a room with men that want me dead. Yes, I've been here before but not quite like this.

# 27.

Sam parks the vehicle in the parking garage without further delay. The car ride was filled with questions from Sam to Eve, going over everything he could, gathering information, trying to debunk her story of things being spiritual or scientific. At first, I enjoyed hearing them speak. Sam would stumble over every word of his hypothesis while Eve calmly spoke with no regard for his so-called life's work. It did get annoying shortly after I noticed Eve getting pissed. She's an incredible being, and while Sam didn't notice or care about her being pestered, I couldn't let it go on for much longer. I typically hate confrontation, but for her, I was willing to put my feelings aside. I never did this for anyone before, but somehow, I think being in the presence of an Astro-projecting, time and space traveling star woman has done something for my confidence. How else could I explain attacking a Gaius with a dozer other than a direct attempt to commit suicide? Of course, I don't have to confront him verbally when I can just divert the conversation. I tried changing the music to spark up some sort of debate between him and me but to no avail. Instead, he simply spoke scientifically about sound waves. Sam is just hellbent on everything science. I too love it but not enough to discuss it for the last leg of a road trip. Between him taking directions from Eve, texting while driving, and sounding like an audiobook for an encyclopedia, I'm almost sure I've finally met someone a tad bit more unusual to have around than me. He finally shuts up when we reached Durham. I've never been here before, and it wasn't the most charming place in the nation. Several office buildings have long been abandoned and desperately in need of a good demolishing team. Eve continues to lead us through the city, and we finally make it to our destination; Evergreen Hospital.

Sam enters the three-story parking garage attached to the side of the medical center, driving to the second layer and finally parking. "I can't believe we actually made it," Eve says, stepping out of the truck and taking in the sight of all the vehicles, inhaling the smog trapped within the layers of the concrete garage. "This will all be over soon, Herman."

After slamming the door shut, I dig my hands in my pockets. "I wouldn't have thought the life that needed saving would be at a hospital if you didn't tell us, Eve. I was expecting a monster truck rally where a driver loses control or maybe a fair ride gone bad, but I just watch too much damn television. Fate seems to make things rather easy for you, Eve, aside from the Gaius who may not be named," I say, taking in the hint of concern across Doctor Samuel's face.

"I'm amazed we made it this far without being shot at or torn to pieces. Hopefully, we can move on with no more interruptions. A shame Sean couldn't make it here. I hope things turn out alright for him even though I know of Victor and the ragtag of killers he's dealing with. Things don't typically turn out that well when they're involved."

Eve simply smiles at me, somehow reassuring me that things would be alright for him. This is Sean aka Hammer we're talking about here. He's been through a lot of scenarios just like this and somehow manages to come out of everything alive. Sean's an even more powerful now thanks to Eve, so he'll be able to take those men apart without any issue. With two hours to spare, we start to make our way to the main facility to save a life and to stop Eve from exploding and potentially becoming a black hole. Sam suddenly stops in his tracks as he checks his cell phone. I freeze too after hearing his loafers screech to a halt on the pavement. Eve continues to walk towards the facility.

"They're here, Herman. I'm sorry that I didn't warn or tell you about them coming here before, but none of that matters now."

I instantly know who he's talking about. "You know, I had my doubts about you, Samuel, and it seems you proven them to be true. Did you tell your people to meet us here?"

"I only told my direct superior, Herman. He was supposed to be the only one to meet us here and witness all this right along with me, but our conversation must have been intercepted." He tosses his cellphone to me, and I catch it effortlessly. "Look at the message he just sent me."

WE'VE BEEN COMPROMISED, SAMUEL. THE TACT TEAM INTERCEPTED US AND IN MORE NUMBERS THAN BEFORE. DON'T ENTER THE PREMISES.

"We have a problem, Eve!" I shout, and she stops in her tracks, looking back at me. I wave the cellphone at her. "Doctor Samuel here accidentally ambushed us, I think. There's a tact team on site here waiting to capture us if we enter the building."

"I'm sure I could dispatch them without concern, but you know what will come if I use my power. We have to think of another way to get around all this and quickly. We don't have much time left, and we already know what may happen if I don't get there in time."

I raise one corner of my mouth into a diabolical smirk and slip Sam's phone into my pocket. He frowns and throws his hands up in the air. "I think I'll hold on to this, considering you got us in this mess in the first place with all your unsecured texting on your government agency phone. You might as well have laid out the red carpet for them to come to us."

Sam scowls at me. "You think I wanted this to happen, Herman? This was not my intention. I just wanted to get this documented in the name of science. I didn't think they would go as far as to track us. They don't even have the authorization to do such. All the highers agreed to let Dr. Carson handle this incident his way, especially after losing and injuring so many after the last task force attack."

"I believe him," Eve intervenes. "We don't have much time to spare. Everything is as it should be, but we must move forward if we are to finish this." She begins to walk towards the entrance of the hospital and Sam follows behind her. My mind frantically attempts to come up with a plan that wouldn't involve Felix showing up and ripping us apart. The only thing that comes to mind is conveniently locating the nurse attire to blend in, but that only works on TV....or does it? I shake the thought out of my head, and then I see two men in tactical gear appear out of the entrance, shoving an older man in business casual clothing outdoors before Sam and Eve could get to it. His arm is bandaged up with a sling to support it.

"We got your warning, Dr. Carson, but it came too late," Samuel says. Dr. Carson exhales in frustration and then adjusts his sling. I notice he is wearing one of the medical doctor's lab coat. He tried to pose as one of the staff. Great minds think alike.

"You didn't think it would be that easy now, did you?" The voice that spoke from behind sends chills through my body. He's armed to the teeth, accompanied by a few other tact team members only a step or so behind him. As he got closer, I could see what his name tap reads on his vest: "Marcus."

# 28.

The men are still gathered around me. Viktor is looking directly at me as if he never took his eyes off me; waiting for me to regain consciousness the whole time. His expression lights up and a grin inches across his pale face.

"You finally came back, Hammer," he says, signaling his men to get ready to begin the assault again. "I want you to be awake to witness all this. I want to see the pain in your eyes as these little sessions of ours gets worse and worse."

My body can still feel a faint pain from the previous beatings, but I can also feel my strength returning, and it wasn't just my normal strength either. I could feel the energy begin to surge through my veins as I begin to heal myself. My body and face still ache, but the recovery sensation is enough to take the edge off. It's as if a natural pain killer comes along with the connection. I need just a little more time before I act, just a little more time to get fully charged. "I know you plan on making me die a horrible death, but I want you to understand something about what happened to your brother, Viktor."

"You're right, Sean. There's nothing you can say that's going to stop the outcome of this day. So just know whatever you say is pointless, and you might as well take it to the grave with-"

"Your brother's death was by his own hands, Viktor. You already know we acquired all his drugs and guns through a hostile takeover, but we offered him a deal at the end. A deal to end the cycle and to join us in the new empire. He didn't take the loss lightly and thought of himself above us. We did rush his home, but not with the intent to kill him. We were there to intimidate him. Instead of complying, he chose never to follow our command, and your brother took his own life." The Russian man stared at me through stunned eyes with his mouth agape. His men stop in their tracks, and they look at me and then him, trying to get a read on what he wants to do from here. Viktor stands from his seat and turns away from me, his hand wiping over his eyes briefly before turning around and glaring at me. He looks to his men and regains his composer with a fix of his black necktie.

"Yes, my brother did believe he was above all, and it does sound like him to do such. However, his death still is a direct result of you and your boss's efforts. Not for just those that resulted in my brother's death, but for my men you and your large friend have injured recently at the gas station the other day. As I said, what you say will change nothing, Hammer. You still will meet your end today," Viktor says, returning to the stone-cold killer persona. "Go on and continue the beating, Axel."

I can feel the power like I did in jail. The pulses of energy coursing throughout my body and making me feel unlike anything I have ever experienced before. "Last chance, guys. Just walk away from my family and me and move on with you-" Axel's fist collides with my jaw, but to his surprise, I'm unaffected. I narrow my gaze and smile, still feeling the minor pain from earlier but no pain from the attack. My attacker sees something different about me before the rest of the room notices.

"I tried to warn you morons and give you a chance to walk away from all this, but now it's too late. I'm going back to my old ways, and all of you are going to need stretchers to get out of here," I say as I snap the handcuffs with ease, catching Axel's fist with one hand and hitting his chest with the other. The blow sends him flying across the room and through the window. The two men standing outside smoking as Axel stops abruptly against the windshield of the parked car, motionless. Everyone freezes and looks at me as I stand slowly with broken handcuffs dangling from my wrists, dried blood caked on my face and shirt, yet appearing to be anew. Another goon attacks me, but his attacks are in slow motion. I dodge them easily and deliver an uppercut to the bottom of his chin. His body flips backward and lands awkwardly against the nightstand before hitting the floor.

"Shoot him, Trevor!" Viktor shouts at the other man standing in the room with us. Trevor reaches into his waistline, grabbing the pistol, and just as he brings it up, I'm in front of him, my hand grasping his wrist. I can feel his bones and ligaments distort and crack as I squeeze tighter. The gun drops from his hand instantly, and Trevor yells in agony. I headbutt him, silencing his scream and rendering his body limp as I turn, swinging his unconscious body to the floor with a spin and release of his wrist. Viktor runs toward the open door as the other three men enter the room. One enters through the door and the other two come in through the open window. Two of them charge at me while the other pulls his gun. In the blink of an eye, I'm standing in front of the gunman, snatching the weapon out of his hand with one hand and slapping him to the ground with the other. Viktor scurries out of the room in a panic, and I wait for the other two to act. One of them takes a step, so I point the gun at him.

"Guns were never my style, fellas. If you haven't noticed yet, I'm more of a hands-on kind of guy," I taunt as I drop the magazine out of the weapon and attempt to crumble the gun like a paper ball. The barrel bends slightly as I winch. "They make it look so much easier in superhero movies."

I turn as I hear a car beginning to back out of the parking lot at maximum throttle. It could be none other than Viktor making his escape. He knows where my family is, and I can't let him get away. I throw the gun and hit the one guy in the face, blood spurts from his nose as he screams out. As soon as he goes down, the last man standing unexpectedly rushes me. He spears me, lifts me into the air, and rushes us both through the window. We tumble out of it and accompany with loud grunts. I roll over backward and sit up on my knees just in time to see something metallic glim out of the corner of my eye before it hits me across my cheek. Brass knuckles were outdated, yet still effective in any street brawl. The pain comes swiftly like the thunder after a close lightning strike. I know from my experiences in fighting that you don't let up on your opponent when you have him right where you want him. He isn't going to let up unless I do something. Still stunned, I lunge and shove my attacker away. He stumbles, losing his balance on the poorly paved parking lot and falls backward. I push the pain to the back of my mind as I scramble and shuffle up the down man and punch him twice for punching me.

As I wearily stand, taking a couple of steps back from the unconscious aggressor, the roar of an engine and screeching tires erupts. I have just enough time to brace for impact as the car bashes into me.

# 29.

My eyes burst open, and my heart is racing. The sound of the tires protesting the pavement still echoes in my head. The impact knocked me back into a room that was not my own, across the bed and against the wall next to the bathroom. Only a few moments could've passed before I regain consciousness. A car door slams shut and a metallic clicking of some kind could be heard. It's none other than Viktor coming to finish the job he started. Thanks to my powers, I manage to take a blow from a vehicle and live, but I'm still in pain from it. My body is healing itself faster than ever, but it still isn't enough. I feel the aches throughout my body, and it leaves me motionless as I sit my back against the wall, waiting for my aggressor to appear in through the same broken window seal I came crashing through. The door kicks open to reveal Viktor standing there with a gun pointing into the room. I quickly lie back down to hide my exact location from him with the bed as my concealment.

"How did you like that you fucking freak?" he says, slowly stepping into the room, looking for my body. "You can take a lot of hurting, Hammer, and that you've always been known to do, but I could never imagine you would be this strong. Maybe your adrenaline kicked in, and you wanted to have one last hoorah before I kill you. Not sure what kind of shape getting hit by that car left you in, but if you are still alive, there's a bonus for you. You get to hear me make a phone call that will send your family straight to hell with you."

My heart skips a beat as the realization of losing them begins to dig into me. The hardest thing to accept is that it's all my own doing. There is no way I can let him do this, but I'm not fully recovered from the crash just yet. Maybe I can buy myself some time to gather the energy needed for a counterstrike. I slide my body up against the wall, making eye contact with Victor. He points the gun at me with a smile.

"Holy fucking shit. You survived all that, Hammer? You are one hard fucker to kill, but I think I have you right where I want you," Viktor gloats. "You are a bloody, bruised mess, and you may think this is the end of the line for you, but not quite yet. You probably hospitalized all my guys, and they are like family to me. They're the only family I got after hearing your bullshit story about my brother offing himself. So, for that, I have to make you pay. I lose my family, and you lose your family that you tried to hide from me, in plain sight, I might add."

I spit blood on the floor next to me as I start to crawl out of the space I'm wedged in, between the bed and nightstand, and I come out into the open. "Leave my family out of all this, Viktor. They never asked for this lifestyle, and I even went as far as keeping them out of your grasp to prove that they have nothing to do with all this. You can do what you have to do to me. I get it. I deserve anything you planned and more. I knew all the things I've done would eventually catch up to me. I always knew that. Even after I told the truth about your brother, I didn't expect you to show mercy. I just wanted you to know what happened. We were enemies to the end, and had it not been for what happened between the two mobs, he may have lived to be here today. However, all our greed boiled over and pent us against each other. I was forced to do a lot of bad things to a lot of good people like your brother's people that I respected. I had to let that respect go because of wartime. After it all ended, I had to walk away from it, but the blood is still on my hands, Viktor. My hands alone. I carry that burden. No one else has to die because of me. Just settle it once and for all, right here."

Viktor stands there for a moment, lowering his gun and glaring at me with a grin on his face. "You are going to pay for what you did but killing you now just doesn't do it for me. I need to break you first. I need you to know that before you die, I killed your family. You left me with nothing in this world, Hammer. A brother is gone. It's only fair for you to feel the same." He takes his cell phone out while pointing his pistol back at me. "Consider this a final fuck you from me to you for my brother, Vince."

With no time to spare, I lunge at Viktor. He notices at the last second and fires a shot into me. I ignore the gunshot as I punch him directly in the face. He shouts in pain as his body slams against the wall next to the room entrance. His gun drops to the floor. The weight of my left arm is just too heavy to use, so I grab his neck with my right hand and shove his body against the wall, lifting him slightly off his feet as he gurgles on the blood in his throat.

"I tried to warn you, but you didn't listen to me, kid! I told you the truth about your brother, and I even took the blame for what happened to him, but I will not take the blame for the death of my family. I can't allow you to do it. Now, if you want to make it out of this alive, you'll tell whoever it is at my house to vacate and take Kevin with them. If one hair is hurt on my family, I'll squeeze your head slowly until it pops like a melon," I say to him assertively before slamming him against the wall again and watching him slouch down to the floor, gasping for air. "Pick up the phone and make the call or I'll end you."

Viktor picks up the phone with one hand while his other hand rubs the redness of his neck. He makes a call with the phone on speaker. The men say where they are and that they are waiting for further instruction. Viktor simply says to call the man outside and snatch him away from my home without harming my family. The goon didn't second guess or question him even though he could hear the hurt in Viktor's voice. He hangs up.

"Slide me the phone," I say to him as I begin to feel woozy and pain starts to stab into the heaviness of my arm. He slides me the phone as ordered, but as I bend to grab it, I start to feel weaker, and I fall backward, taking a seat on the floor across from Viktor. I could feel a distant power pulling in my mind. The feeling felt all too familiar. It's Eve; she's activating her powers. I can feel her anger surrounded by doubt and fear. It is now that I realize I'm sitting in my own pool of dark blood streaming from my shoulder, down my arm, and to the floor. Viktor shot me when the gun went off, but I didn't realize it until now. The feeling of Eve's emotions and power usage begin to fade as I succumb to all the aches and pains of my mortality. My body is still trying to heal itself slowly, but the damage I've taken during these few minutes are just too dire. My blood loss is evidence of that, and I begin to feel weary.

"Looks like all that heroic impossible shit you pulled is starting to take its toll on you, flapjack," Viktor mocks. "I admit, I have never seen anything like what you did here, but weird shit has been happening this weekend, considering what your other friend did to my crew at the gas station," he says as he reaches down to his ankle and pulls a knife from a small sheath. He can see the weakness starting to set in as my eyes begin to blink slower and slower. I turn over to my stomach as I begin to drag myself across the floor, making my escape from him. He gets up on his feet with the assistance of the wall and steps toward me.

"You can't escape my revenge, shithead. I'm going to carve you up and gut you like the animal you are and then I'm going to tell my boys to handle that sexy wife of yours."

I could've dealt with my death but not the death of my family. I stop struggling to low crawl and hide my free hand under my chest. Viktor grabs me by the shoulder. "Turn around. I want me to be the last thing you see before you die." He slowly turns me over to my back as his other hand raises to jam the knife in my chest. That's when he sees the gun pointing at him.

Two gunshots ring out and blood spurts from Viktor's chest. His eyes shut, and he slumps backward awkwardly. He got careless and forgot about his gun that he dropped when I bashed him against the wall. I drop the gun and lay my head back as I feel my consciousness beginning to fade away. I can hear the phone ringing from the other room.

# 30.

Marcus kicks the back of my knee, causing me to kneel as the rest of the men get in positions around us. His hand grasps my shoulder as he signals for another soldier to grab Eve. A female comes with a pistol in hand and sticks it up to her head. Her nametape reads "Michelle". Eve doesn't look worried or concern at the implied gesture, so I turn my attention to the doctors that put us in this mess, to begin with. They were also being detained and held at gunpoint. This is starting to look more like an unsanctioned action by the second.

"Where's that friend of yours that killed Reese?" The female soldier with the buzzcut asks as she becomes more aggressive, shoving Eve's head with the barrel of the pistol. "We unburied his body the next day after the officials cleared the place as if he was buried alive and now you will be too if you don't tell us where Felix and Sean are."

"There's nothing you can do here to make me give you that information," Eve sternly replies, looking at her from the corner of her eyes. "Even if you were to locate either of them, you wouldn't be able to take them with force. Sean's connection is not complete, but you saw what he could do already. And concerning Felix, he's what is called a Gaius and has been one with Earth for centuries. He is powered by the spirit of the planet. If you think your weapons will have any effect on such a creature, you are mistaken. He would destroy us all if he were to appear here."

Eve is right, but I don't think the group we are dealing with is the kind to take heed to any warnings. I look up at the dozen men around us, all with hate and the flames of vengeance in their eyes. Then I peer up at Marcus who gives the female a nod. She bashes Eve over the shoulder with the bottom of the pistol. She stumbles forward before the soldier pushes her to the ground.

"Our patience is running thin, woman. Shell needs answers right now, or there will be bloodshed. It doesn't have to come to this, yet. We can spare you until we get what we want and turn all of you in for our doctors here to study. I'm sure they're dying to know what makes the alien tick," Marcus yells to Eve as Shell continues to assault her. Eve collapses to the ground. The star lady shows no signs of pain or anguish on her face. Being who she is and knowing what would happen, she can never use her power. If she does, that will attract what none of us really want to see. The evil Captain Planet; the monster, Felix. Shell stands up and takes a large inhale.

"You're a lot tougher than you look, bitch. I haven't heard as much as a whimper from you. You're barely even bruised. How much punishment can you take?" The soldier says. She then kicks Eve's midsection while she is sitting up on all fours. Eve's back curves upward, and she rolls over to her side, releasing the air in her lungs and coughing. I've had all I can take of seeing her bashed this way. I'm no Hammer or anything of the sort, but I can't just stand by and watch Eve get handled like this, regardless of her being a spiritual galactic anomaly.

"That's enough!" I shout at Shell. "All of this you are doing is suicide. You may have bigger guns, a false strength in numbers, and stronger resolve than ever, but none of this even matters. You can beat her senseless, which could take longer than you can imagine, but in the end, even if Felix does come here, we are all doomed. You've seen the damage he can do. You've seen the mayhem and destruction he can cause firsthand. There's no way you could think that anything you do now can change that. He's far beyond our comprehension. Tell them Sam, you worthless piece of crap. This is all your fault."

"He is half right, Captain Marcus. After encountering him two times and seeing him dispatch trained killers with ease, I don't think bringing him to this hospital is the best course of action. I don't agree with this being my fault though, Herman, or being a piece of crap. I didn't purposely lure us here into this unsanctioned trap. You may want to consult Dr. Carson on that. He's the one who spilled the beans," Samuel snaps back at me and darts a quick eye at the doctor who's seen better days.

Dr. Carson clears his throat before he begins to speak. "Gentlemen look at me. My face is battered, and my arm in this sling isn't me making a fashion statement. I've been shot and beaten by the same people responsible for this. Obviously, I had no choice in the matter if I wanted to remain alive. This is truly your fault, Herman. Had you brought your impervious friend, Sean, here with you, I'm almost certain that the probability of this outcome happening would be null. So the argument you both make are valid, but we wouldn't be in this predicament at all if he wasn't-"

"Enough of the bullshit!" Marcus yells. "I give two shits about your arguments. We are here now, and we want both of your friends to show. Either you tell us where they are, or you contact them and bring them to us. One way of the other, we are going to get what the hell we want no matter what you think the outcome of this will be." He catches my angry stare and hits the side of my face with the buttstock of his rifle. I could feel the swelling start as I taste the blood from my damaged gums. I lay here on the floor, holding my face and regretting that I said anything at all.

"Don't you touch him. He has nothing to do with what you are asking for here," Eve says before Shell delivers a boot to her face.

"You give us what we want, and none of this has to happen this way. You'll save yourselves a lot of pain and a lot of problems. Tell her where they are!" Marcus pulls me up by the back of my t-shirt and signals another soldier over. He punches the other side of my face, and I fall over again, spitting blood out of my mouth.

"Stop it, I said. You're making a grave mistake." Eve screams as Shell places a boot on her back, stopping her from getting up.

"Looks like we may have found a soft spot in her armor, captain," she says. "She can take lots of punishment but doesn't seem to be able to handle her friend over there getting hit. I don't think that's her boyfriend. I'm sure she would want someone much tougher than that softy.

The captain lifts me from the ground again while I'm still holding my face which feels as if it's going to fall off. His soldier punches me square in the face, my nose giving in and a slight stream of blood begins to trickle from my nostril. I want to tell Eve not to give in, but me screaming in agony drowns out my notions of being a tough guy. Suddenly, I could see a light shining from across the parking garage. The assault on my face had come to a halt as everyone pauses to see

Eve in her true state. Her skin illuminates, and her third eye opens on her forehead. Shell stumbles away from her, bewildered. We were so close to making it, but our chances of making the deadline just became slim now that Felix will be here any second.

# 31.

The whole time we've been traveling together, I never saw this look in Eve's eyes. Her skin is brighter than ever, and her three eyes were illuminating a fierce red – an obvious sign that she has no patience left. I sit up to my knees and take in the look of all the surprise faces that are witnessing her true form. Most of the soldiers are left astonished while others were rubbing their eyes, trying to make sure what they were seeing wasn't an illusion. The look of those around us didn't concern me much, except the look of fear from Shell as she sat on the floor, peering up at her so-called prisoner, helpless to what she is going to do next. There is one that still stands there unshaken. His resolve for the death of his comrade and subordinate left him with a streak of bravery and more confidence. It's Marcus. He shows no fear at the amazing sight of the true Eve.

"I've had enough of the light show. Somebody shoot this bitch!" he shouts. None of his men respond. He repeats himself but louder, jolting the men back to reality as some of them shuffle to aim their weapons. His female counterpart rolls to safety as they all begin to make their way to the front of Eve so as not to catch Michelle in their crossfire. I look at the scientist and his apprentice as they just stand and marvel at what Eve can do. I see them cover their ears, reminding me that the firing is about to begin. Realizing that I'm too close to the action, I turn away and start to crawl from the dangers of everything that comes with a gunfight in the middle of a parking garage. My shirt is tugged on violently, and I have no choice except to stop in my tracks. I didn't even look up to know that Marcus didn't want me to miss out on what is about to happen.

He has no idea.

The first burst of rounds goes off, signaling screams of surprise from the other floors and any other bystander that was in the immediate area. Eve seems to be standing in the spot she has been in, but she isn't. She moves to the soldier that fired upon her so fast that an afterimage of her still standing in her previous spot is just now moving towards him. She grabs the barrel of his rifle, and it instantly turns fire red, burning his hands and melting the weapon. She slaps him and he yelps like a wounded dog while he falls to his knees, holding his cheek. She moves on to the next, leaving another after image for us to behold as she continues to work on the next man with the same amount of effort and precision. I look at the first man, and the skin on his face is singed away, revealing burned flesh. Before I can look up at the next, she's already made her rounds. Most of the men were down and incapacitated, no longer willing to fight what she really is.

"What the hell is happening to them?" Michelle screams out as she looks around the garage, catching mere glimpses of Eve as she moves through the area without so much as a scrap. You can still hear gunfire while she moves, but neither I nor the soldiers could identify which afterimage of her is really her. Shell runs over to Marcus and me, waiting on him to make his next move.

"Fall back, Michelle. We have to come up with another way to handle the situation and this fucker right here."

"Fucker right here? Oh, you're talking about me. Sorry, but if you haven't noticed-" He slaps the side of my head with an open palm, ending my witty comeback.

"You've done enough talking for one lifetime, don't you think?" Michelle says as she grabs my arm.

"Follow me. We'll be able to get some distance, regroup, and come up with some sort of plan," Marcus says. They both grab hold of my appendages and drag me further into the parking garage.

***

I could hear the shouts and screams from above, but nothing is being said on the radio. Not only did they find the targets they were looking for, but they are already engaging by the sounds of it. My orders were to keep a lookout here in the lobby, making sure the targets don't show up through the front entrance. It would be stupid to enter here, but you never know what's going on in the mind of a fugitive. The captain told me to stand down and dress casually to blend in. I have my handgun on me, but given my orders, I'm not supposed to engage. Just log and report any activity from the suspects we are after that are responsible for the loss of lives and the solar flare incident that happened yesterday. I take one more hit from my cigarette and throw it to the ground. I pull out my radio, ready to call in to see if they need my help above when out walks a massive man from a large patch of decorative bushes that were planted alongside the walkway leading up to the lobby entrance. He walks toward the entrance with a sense of purpose, and his head tips upward where the action could be heard from. A slight smile appears on his face as he continues to make his way inside.

Then it comes to me. I swipe left two times on my phone and got eyes on one of the targets we are looking for. According to the information we got from the eggheads, this is Felix. I look at him as he approaches and take note of how much more massive, he is in person. I'm almost half his size and given what he did to the previous sergeant and a few others, I can't take him on with just my pistol. My best bet is to radio in what I see as I'm ordered to do. He reaches the entrance of the hospital when he notices me standing off to the side. He pauses his stride, head still facing forward, takes a step backward, and finally turns his head to look at me. The turn was slow yet intimidating like a statue slowly coming to life. I ease my hand into my coat pocket, placing it slowly on my pistol.

"You shouldn't litter. Our planet is in enough stress as it is already, and I don't need you adding to that problem," Felix informs me with his voice that sends trembles through my body.

"What are you referring to, sir?" I ask him, trying to stop my voice from cracking as I respond to him.

"You are standing on a cigarette which is not biodegradable. Let this be the last time you do that, or you'll have to face the consequences for your actions. Many of you damage my land without thinking of the long-term consequences of your actions. My primary function isn't to prevent you all from littering and polluting; however, I won't let you perform such an action in my presence. I'm not here for you, but I can be," Felix replies.

I remember what my orders were and take my hand out of my pocket. I lift my foot and pick up my cigarette butt as he requested with a nervous smile. The look of seriousness never leaves his face. Felix turns his head and continues his stride through the hospital doors. I release a large sigh as I walk over to the trash can and throw away the butt. I didn't realize I was holding my breath until now.

"Only observe and report," I say to myself. "No need to attack him if my orders don't dictate to do such," I say as I wipe the beads of sweat from my forehead and reach for my radio.

# 32.

I open my eyes to a dark sky, but everything around me is still visible as if there is daylight. I'm lying on my back in the field of high grass, observing it as the wind blows causing the peacefulness of the field to begin to ripple like the surface of a lake, touched by the wind. Sitting up, I attempt to remember where I am and how I got here, but the memory feels so faint. As if whatever happened, happened decades ago if it even happened at all. I can somehow, feel it all slipping away from my grasp. Everything that happened before now, didn't really happen to me, did it? It all feels like a lucid dream that I watched from another vantage point.

"You think time and space are two different things. That's such a mortal way of thinking."

The grass around me dies as the wind slows to a stop. It all loses its color as if the cold of winter had come in an instant. My world starts to crumble underneath me. It all makes sense to me. I know that I'm dying, but I can't remember why. I know that I have reached a higher plateau than others, however, it's not enough for the condition my body is in right now. Death is about to take me.

"We are connected to the universe around us and the one beyond us, Sean." A voice echoes from overhead.

The land around me begins to shift as this world begins to die. The dead grass collapses upon itself in splotches and becomes baron; only dirt is left in its wake as the land rumbles violently. Parts of the ground start vaulting into the air, broken apart by the earthquake that continues to destroy the peace around me. Other parts of the land are sinking into the earth, giving away to my despair.

The ground beneath me stops rumbling, nor does it sink into itself or vault into the sky. I stand to my feet looking at the catastrophe around me. I can feel rising anger and fear away from what is happening here, but those emotions are not my own. I even feel inclined to help but can't grasp who or what needs help. It's hard to differentiate these senses anymore.

"Is this what dying feels like? A handful of distant thoughts and overwhelming confusion? What's happening?" I say out loud to myself.

"I can't help you complete your connection. Everyone is different and you must do this step alone," the voice speaks again.

I'm coming apart. All these things are happening around me, causing my focus to fade. The world crumbles under my feet. I can't help, but wonder if I am already dead?

"We all have a star in the universe that represents our souls. Once you realize this and can connect yourself to it, you'll be able to be who you truly are."

Everything falls away and I am alone in silence, floating amongst complete darkness. Without all the mayhem going on around me, my brain starts to reel in what is happening to me. My physical body has lost so much blood that I can't even sustain my inner realm. This is bad. Through it all, I can still feel Eve's essence. She's using her power for whatever reason and I know she needs me. How can I be her protector if I'm dead? I can't let this end this way. It would be so easy to give in to this darkness and rest forever, but one thing about who I really am and that's the fact that I don't go down so easy. I'm not ready to give in to the nothingness of death. This place is where we all come through death, but I'm not dead. Not yet.

"We all have to do our part to make the universe go around. We all have a role in this, and you are no different."

Suddenly, I'm back in my collapsing inner realm. I manage to buy myself more time by coming back here. Something feels different. Even with the earth I'm standing still shifting, I feel a sense of stability within myself. All my life, from my childhood, I've lived in unstable environments; from an abusive home to an even more aggressive adulthood. I was bringing pain to others because I couldn't bear the pain of what I had become. Now, feeling this stability, I am becoming something else. New life simmers underneath the surface of the skin of what I was before all this. My eyes close and the darkness that surrounded me returns, but I fight and open them again. It hurts now to be away from the darkness of death, but if I can just hold on a little longer, things will be different. The last part of my world crumbles away and I jump, taking a leap of faith into what is now outer space. It feels like I am standing, but I'm not at all. I'm simply floating. I turn around and watch as my world collapses onto itself. I can see the memories of the thing that made up my planet, burn away in brilliant bright flashes and sparkling colors. All my violence, selfishness, and greed consume by a massive implosion of swirling fires.

"You'll find who you truly are here, among the stars."

A part of me wanted to swoop down there and save the remnants of my former self, but I know going back now will only be the death of me and the disappointment of those that depend on me. The cosmos consumes what is left of my world leaving me, homeless and alone in space.

# 33.

The barrel of Marcus's gun is being pressed against the temple of my head. Michelle and Marcus managed to drag me across the parking lot, close enough to see the stairs down to the next floor. They were too busy running away with me in tow while I was watching Eve do away with the rest of their entourage.

"Stop," she says after dispatching with the last of their men. They both turn to see her celestial body shimmering and changing colors as if you are looking at a star in the night sky through a telescope – distant but close at the same time.

"You come any closer, I'll blow his fucking brains out!" the captain threatens. The feeling of the gun against my temple, trembling lightly tells me that he's very serious about what he says. Shell holsters her pistol and unslings her rifle. She opens a circular compartment attached to the underside of the barrel. She loads a round inside and slams the compartment close. She stands firm as she takes aim in front of us.

"Just keep moving, Marcus. I'll handle this my way once and for all. It's clear that our bullets are no match for this thing, but let's see how she fairs against explosive rounds," Shell says.

"Captain! The other target you are waiting for is here, and he's on his way to you right now as we speak," a voice reports over the radio. Marcus only looks at the radio attached to his shoulder but doesn't bother to answer it. He knows his plate is already full and handling another thing like her at the same time would be suicide. Deep down, I hope the target the soldier reported about is Sean, but I know better. That would be too convenient for us and this whole trip has been anything but that. Without a doubt in my mind, I know that it is Felix.

THUNK!

The noise yells out right before the impact. It rattles the parking garage as it sends pebbles and debris in every direction. Car alarms were sounding off.

"We don't have time to be fucking around with this spacewoman. We have bigger fish to fry coming our way any second now," she replies while dropping the expended bullet shell and grabbing another from a small bag on her waistline.

"There are still civilians in the area, and that breaks the protocol if any of them are harmed. All the other federal agencies will have a field day with this if this turns out badly," Marcus says, his vengeance finally giving away to his responsibility.

"Protocol went out the window when that thing killed Reese, Marcus. We broke the law getting this information from the scientists, and we definitely are not allowed to be here given all those circumstances along with no order being issued to do so, but here we fucking are!" she yells at him angrily. She begins to scan the area as the smoke starts to clear from the blast, looking for the remains of Eve.

It was then I realize that the two researchers weren't responsible for this little fiasco. I wonder if they managed to take cover once all the sparks started to fly. Sitting on the pavement, I scan the place alongside the two soldiers, looking for any movement at all.

"When will you understand that your weapons are useless against me?" Eve's voice echoes eerily through the garage.

"Eve! Just go and complete the task at hand. We came this far, and if you don't get there soon, Felix will be here and then it's all over," I yell before Marcus kicks me to the pavement and stomps my rib cage.

"If you leave here, he dies now," Marcus spouts.

"Herman," Eve's voice whispers to me. This is not where you end, and I must protect that. Besides, you have been a great guardian substitute, and where would I be without you?"

Looking up, I see her appear in front of Michelle, shoving her. She soars across the parking garage, slamming into the concrete wall, making a loud grunt. By the time Marcus lays his eyes back on Eve, she's already gone again. He lets off a volley of shots from his pistol, hitting nothing. His fear finally takes control. He breaks away from me, dropping his pistol and swinging up his rifle. He fires it in every direction. My fear surfaces, and it overcomes the sharp pain in my side, allowing me to crawl behind the nearest vehicle.

The shooting comes to an end after a loud bang and a cracking sound. The captain's bloodcurdling scream can vouch for my thought of something being severely broken. There's another large thump and silence. Marcus' body descends from a blow from Eve, and he finally comes to rest on the hood of the very car I'm hiding next to. I'm not sure if he's dead or alive, but out of a feeling of revenge, I shove his limp body to the floor, and his face slams into the ground. It feels wrong yet satisfying.

"That's for all the unnecessary manhandling you did to me," I say as I kick his body and almost fall in the process. I exchange a quick gaze with the celestial form of Eve. A slight smile appears on her face, and I want to smile back at her, but I'm frozen. I can't even get the words out, but she already knows what's happening to me. Her smile vanishes just as quickly as it appeared, and she turns to look at what I am seeing.

Felix.

"You made it this far without so much an inkling of your power being used, and I have to say, I'm impressed. Others that were able to get to where you are weren't as smart as you, star, and I do compliment you for that too, but unfortunately for you, I can't let this play out any further."

"A life hangs in the balance of all this, Felix. I know you mean well-"

"Enough! I won't let you exist here anymore, poisoning others with your celestial ways and energies. You've done enough damage here, and I'll make sure this is where it ends, once and for all. I'm not exactly sure which body you are trying to reach, and it did puzzle me at first, but now I know the answer; if I live, you must die. An entity like you is a god amongst men, and you threaten the course of life for everyone here. It's my responsibility to keep things even. To keep the world godless until fate deems it so. You have interjected in the lives of others enough. Now you meet your reckoning."

Felix begins to make his approach to Eve. Knowing that there is no other way, she stands her ground. However, I'm sure she already knows that if she doesn't get help, this will end badly for her.

# 34.

With no gravity to keep me grounded, I glide aimlessly, into space, my own consciousness releasing its hold. Here, there is no sound. I start to feel something tug at my body as I slowly drift further away from the crumbs of my vanquished planet. I can't tell which way is up or down as the tugging sensation continues to pull me. I turn my attention to what I'm drifting towards. A black hole, spiraling into nothingness. Realizing I don't have much time left before venturing into the hole, I start to reflect, helping myself come to terms with my true death.

This isn't just the end of me, but also the end of all the suffering I caused others. This will put an end to all the pain I gave to a wife that didn't deserve it; to a daughter that only wanted my love and attention.

The stars contour, twist, and unite, forming Jasmine's and Jada's faces as the gravity of nonexistence continues to drag me to it. At this moment, I see another planet, also beginning to crumble just as mine did, but much slower. The planet is an aqua color with star clusters swirling around it in cosmic rings. The more I investigate it, the more I can feel Eve. It's the connecting gateway that allows us to communicate. I can almost make out her faint whispers to me, but I'm too weary to hear them.

"I owe you an apology, Eve," I say, unsure she can hear me. "You put your time and energy into me and in the end, I let you down. I couldn't save you. I couldn't save the life you wanted me to help you with. I wasn't even able to save myself."

I am the key to all of this. Once I die, all of this goes with me. Still, it is amazing that I came this far. It's clear that many people go their whole lives never knowing what powers are locked away inside.

The black hole draws closer. So close that I can see raw, dead earth floating around it, swirling on the rims of darkness. Even being this close, there are still parts of the swirling matter that sparkle with deep purple and white beauty. My heart starts to beat rapidly, anticipating the cold nothingness that awaits beyond. Is this truly how I die? Succumbing to the faults of Eve, the one to blame for putting me in this predicament.

"No," I say to myself out loud watching my breath in the coldness of space.

This isn't her fault, Sean. It's yours. Stop blaming all your choices and decisions on other people. It wasn't my abusive father that walked me into the doors of the mafia, I did that myself. Kevin didn't take my wife and child from me; I gave them away with my actions. It wasn't Eve that abandon me in this hotel. That's all my own doing.

My head tilts in the direction of the hole.

"I created this end, but it doesn't have to be this way," I whisper as I become part of the debris, floating near the hole. "This is my universe, but it's filled with bad decisions that I created. It's time to make some positive ones. If I must fall into oblivion, then at least I can make peace with it all before I go." I raise my hand towards the darkness, and I stop instantly. The dead matter and balls of light continue their motion, revolving slower now as I turn to see the ruins made by my own faults. The face of my ex-wife and daughter made of stars begin to shed tears.

My family. You never needed me to be happy and for some reason, I never saw that. It was me that needed to make you suffer because I still suffered from my past. That was my way of showing love. That's not love at all. Please forgive me.

Their sadness instantly vanishes as their face outline vacuums onto itself and without a sound, an implosion occurs revealing a new planet. I watch it as it slowly begins to spin on its axis. Incredible. The realization of what just occurred begins to ease my thoughts and gives birth to an entirely different way of thinking.

"If I can create new worlds here, then this means I am the sole ruler of this universe. The god of my inner cosmos. I must accept the blame led on by all my previous actions from the past and through the future," I say as I turn to face the blackhole chasm behind me. I can feel something pulling within me. It's like I'm making my own gravitational force and with it, I push away from the nothingness of death.

"I'm not ready to die because I have so much work to do. So many things left undone and other things to make right." The black hole is now in the distance. I come to the planet that signifies my connection with Eve. Reaching out to it, I can feel it in pain. She needs my help more than ever and I will not let her down. "I know how to seek you out, Eve, and I will once I'm done here.

New planets begin to form all around the galaxy. They loom in mystery, yet I know they are a direct extension of my consciousness. "If my mind can create new worlds, then surely, I can reconstruct an old one, but enriched with hope."

I raise my hands, directed in the location my planet once was that Eve helped me create in the beginning. I move my fingers as if puppeteering pieces of space debris, forcing them to come together under sheer willpower. As the pieces connect, they grow vast, spreading wild and quick, connecting to the other growing pieces. In seconds, the planet is anew. The world has become something different. From here, I can see bodies of waters that accompany the open grasslands. I am the master of my own time and space. Everything that occurs in my life, good or bad, is my fault. The past no longer has a hold on me, nothing in the present is attached to me, and I lead the way to my own destiny. I turn to the black hole so far in the distance and I raise my hand to it.

"I no longer need this darkness in the center of my universe. Instead of living in the dark, I will bask in the light. The darkness fades away as the space matter floating about merges together and in a flash that engulfs the galaxy, the sun is born. The coldness of space is no more. Suddenly, my hands become transparent, signaling me to look at my entire body as it all becomes transparent. It's as if my body is made of the universe itself. The outline of my body incases distant stars, near planets, and the sun. I spin, gracefully, to peer at my Home planet through my left hand's transparency. As I look through the hand, I can see my Home planet, drifting slowly upward, toward my forearm. A heavy breeze distracts me from my observation, causing me to examine my surroundings. Now, I stand in the very field this all began in. The planet made anew by me. High grass blows in waves as the wind moves, causing small ripples over the surface of a clearwater lake in the distance.

"I did it. I've completed the final step," I say aloud, studying my new body made of the galaxy that's been hidden within me. "I never felt this much power before. This is what Eve wanted to happen. This is what connecting to the universe within feels like." I could feel her desperation as if it were my own. This newly awakened self has bonded our emotions as if we were the same being. Setting my sights on the blue, cloudless sky above, I can see her aqua planet as if it was the moon. Slowly, I begin to levitate away from the grasslands.

"You will live to fight another day, Eve," I say as I fly into space. Now, in this new state of being, I understand how time, distance, and space are all equal and are all parallel. I know I can travel through them all simultaneously. There are blurs and distortions in the environment around me as if the sunlight were shining in through the surface of the water. I know these areas in the universe have always been here, just unseen by the disconnected. With my eyes truly opening for the first time, I can see the beauty of it all as I race towards the aquaplanet in distress to aid the one, I'm bound to protect.

# 35.

She had already made herself clear that she was no match for Felix. I saw the painful truth back when he found us in the police station, and it's starting to rear its ugly head, again. Eve attacks were indeed fast enough to avert his counter strikes, but she could only keep it up for so long. His attacks were fierce and powerful. Felix's speed can't match Eve's as she jumps from car to car, dashing away from his strikes. He finally manages to grab her ankle while she moves, clipping her in midair and causing her to sprawl on the hood of a car. Felix grabs her calf with both hands and twirls around. Her helpless body spins with him before colliding with the neighboring car's windshield. The thud of the impact and cracking of the windshield sends waves of nausea through my stomach.

"There is no use in fighting me, star. You and I both know how this will end for you despite your effort," he says as she melts through the rest of the windshield, attempting to get some distance so she could get back on her feet. She kicks the backdoor off the car and jumps to the next car. In a flash, she is behind him, but out of his immediate reach. Felix notices her and braces for an attack, but she isn't there to strike him. Eve takes a glance at him before her head turns toward the hospital entrance doors. She makes a beeline for them, but Felix takes the car she was just in with ease and slings it across the parking lot with a grunt that makes my bones shiver. She stops her advance and dives out of the way immediately. The car hits the ground of the parking garage, twisting long ways and slamming into the automatic doors. They even open before the car smashes into them, jamming into the entrance. It was his plan all along. Now she wouldn't be able to simply outrun him, but she would have to take time to navigate through or around the car. It would be enough time for him to close the distance between them.

"I know what all of you do once you realize you can't win, but escaping me today isn't an option," Felix mocks. "You were better off using your little blinding technique you use before, but even that wouldn't work on me this time. I was busy dealing with your so-called guardian, but not this time. This time, star, you have my full attention." Felix rushes toward her. Her eyes glow red, and so does her hands. She has no other choice but to fight her way out of the scenario.

"I didn't come all this way to fail, Gaius," she shouts as she marches toward him. She begins to trout, and as they meet, Felix swings his boulder-like fist, but she goes around him using her maximum speed, almost appearing to go through him. Eve turns around swiftly and slaps his side, using the same strike that burned the skin of several soldiers earlier. Felix flinches and grunts before kicking her away with a quick sidekick. She flies through the air before tumbling on the ground and rolling. Her defeat is starting to bring tears to my eyes. We've been traveling together only a few days, but it feels like a lifetime. Seeing how she only had three days to live, it was a lifetime. Watching her take this abuse hurts my heart.

"We have to do something," a familiar voice says to me, startling me as I hide behind the car. It's Samuel and Doctor Carson at the rear of the same car. They managed to sneak their way to me through all the battling and without a scratch.

"What can we do, Sam? If she is no match for him, then what exactly are we to do here?" I ask.

"Maybe we can use that soldier's weapon there to attack him?" Dr. Carson chimes in, rubbing his injured arm.

His idea sparks a plan in my head. Now I get why it takes a room full of scientists to crack the codes of life. "You're right, Dr. Carson. I need one of you to distract him and lure him away from Eve while I grab the other rifle Michelle was using before Eve handled her. The rifle she uses has that grenade launcher attached. It probably wouldn't cause enough damage to him, but maybe it will give her the opening she needs to escape." I look and still see Michelle's body lying motionless a mere three cars or so away. "Seeing how your colleague isn't mission capable, you're up Sam."

Sam tries to protest but only ends up swallowing loud enough for us both to hear.

153

"You must help her, Samuel. We are the reason she's in this mess, to begin with, and it's our responsibility to help her live."

Eve screams out in pain before another large crash. We all stop in our tracks. I peek over the hood and see her sliding off the side of a vehicle. The glow she once had illuminating from her body is beginning to give way to all her injuries.

"She's at the end of her line. Take that rifle and use it, Sam," I demand.

"I've never fired a firearm in my life, Herman. Who's to say I won't accidentally hit you?"

"The time for talking is over!" Dr. Carson shouts unforgivingly at his prodigy. If you can't do it yourself, then do it for the name of science just as I did when we met Felix. You must stand up, if not for yourself, then for the answers we seek. If she dies here, then all we've done up until now, including me getting shot, would all be for nothing. We can't let this end as an unsolved mystery, Samuel. Do what you can to see this experiment through."

Samuel stares at Dr. Carson. Something he said must have struck gold. You can see the new-found determination in his eyes.

"For Science," Sam says. He stands up and rushes over to Marcus's gun. I make my way to the rear of the car and dash towards Michelle's weapon. I make it to the last car and see the open space between me and her rifle when a gunshot rings out. It's then I hear the sirens of the squad cars below, but I didn't have time to think about that. The shot caught Felix's attention, stopping his movement to Eve and turning his brow to Sam who isn't hitting anything at all, but it is distracting him long enough for me to grab the weapon.

"I remember you," Felix says as he laughs. "I let you live along with your older friend in the woods, days ago. I should've reconsidered that choice," Felix says as he begins to stomp his way to Sam. Eve is barely conscious, so he has time to squash a bug like him. I rush out into the open area to line myself up with Felix just right.

"I still owe you for what you did to me yesterday, shithead," I say as he stops and turns to see me. Dr. Carson signals Sam to follow him out the rear door leading to the stairs, taking cover from any blowback of this explosion. I brace myself as I pull the trigger.

THUNK!

A small explosion follows as it hits. Smoke pours throughout the garage again, and I know the blast isn't enough to kill Felix, so I act fast. I drop the weapon and move to aid Eve. Her celestial body is beaten and bruised, and a white, blood-like substance streams down from the side of her head. I don't think it's sweat. She opens her eyes and smiles at me.

"We have to get you out of here before this gets worse, Eve. We still have some time before the night is over and maybe we can regroup and…" My voice is silenced by his footsteps which is slowly causing the ground to vibrate.

"You little shits are really starting to piss me off. I didn't come here to kill the likes of you, but you all are giving me no choice with your attacks on me, clearly disrespecting my works to protect the planet from the likes of her and to protect mankind from those who wish to be gods. I can no longer tolerate any of you preventing what must be done here, and now you all will meet the same fate as her."

Fear makes my whole body feel limp. I didn't expect him to recover so quickly, but I should have calculated as such. Suddenly, the car that is blocking the entrance into the hospital begins to slide loudly against the cement. The front end of the vehicle begins to angle away from the entrance as if the entire car is swinging open like a bedroom door, clearing the way into the hospital. Although the smoke is still lingering in the air, I could see a figure standing there in tattered, blood-soaked clothing. The silhouette moves forward showing his face; I can recognize it anywhere.

"Hammer".

# 36.

"Looks like the party got started without me," I say as I take in all the damage and mayhem around the parking garage. Herman is by Eve's side, sitting her up as he looks over at me, sighing with relief.

"Better late than never," Herman says with a hint of amusement in his voice. Judging by his bruises, Herm got his fair share of the action, again. I'll make him pay for that. My eyes are set on Felix who is directly across the garage from me. I start towards him.

"I guess I see why we lost contact for a while there, Eve, but I'm here now. I'm sorry I let you down before, but this time," I pause, then continue, "this time will be different." She simply nods in agreement, too weak to respond any other way.

"I never doubted you for a minute, Sean. I've always known you could overcome anything," she says faintly.

A thunderous chuckle is let out from Felix. "So, you're back for more? I thought you learned your lesson the first time, but I see some of you humans are much harder to teach than others. Don't you move, star, I'll finish your pawn off once and for all and finally deal with you."

I walk past my friends with only a glance before returning my eyes to Felix. "Get her out of here and to the life that she's here to save. I'll deal with this." Felix shakes his head with a smile on his face as if my words were comical.

"I must commend you for your bravery after what I did to you the first time, but there will be nothing here to save you from my full wrath. Here is where you will die, pawn." Felix walks over to meet me face to face. Our eyes lock, and his smile never fades as I look up at him with determination in my eyes.

"Goodbye, weakling," Felix swings at me and I stop the punch with one arm. His smile diminishes only to be replaced by a look of surprise as I close my eyes and open my third eye in the center of my forehead, reopen my other eyes, and deliver a punch to his jaw with my free hand. The Gaius's head snaps back, reeling, leaving him open for my other hand to uppercut his chin, making him more dazed. I finish off with a foot to his midsection, making him stumble back, tripping over a huge pothole in the pavement, falling backward, and rolling over to his stomach.

"He did it, Herman. He completed his connection within, and now he can fight a Gaius, blow for blow," I heard Eve say while Herm is helping her get to her feet. I watch Felix push his upper body up to one knee, wiping the blood from his lower lip with fury in his gaze.

"Did you like that, Felix? Things are going to be much different this bout. That's for beating up on my friends, but the rest is all for my enjoyment," I say to him as he gets up to his feet. Herman and Eve are on their way out as he charges at me. I stand my ground. We begin to exchange blows and parries, fighting like two men that have been fighting their entire lives. I no longer fear him or feel inferior to what he is. I am beyond him now.

He hits me with a left hook, causing me to stumble off in a spin. He delivers a boot to my back that sends me flipping over the front of a nearby car. His attacks still pact a punch, but with my newfound connection, I'm able to recover quicker than I ever have. I jump up and over the hood of the car, vaulting over it and drop kicking him with both legs extended. My back slams against the hood and he pushes away from me, pausing to recover.

"You've been fighting and killing stars for centuries, Felix, but you've never fought someone quite like me before," I say, rolling off the car and taking up a fighting stance.

"Never one quite as sloppy as you are, pawn," he replies. "Yet, you are all the same. As I told you before, you let this star sell you on power and greed of what you can become, not knowing this will make you a sworn enemy of the planet. You are fighting against nature, wanting to save the life of someone that has reached their end. It is not natural to be what you are or for them to live. Therefore, you will be eliminated just like that star."

"Say what you will, but fate has chosen me to save a life. Before this, I've always been about myself and causing harm to others for my own cause. I may be a pawn to you but now is my chance to make things right. For once, I get to use the only thing I've ever been good at, to help do something good."

"Enough of your false self-righteousness!" Felix shouts before continuing his assault.

\*\*\*

I round the corner with Eve draped on my shoulder after getting off the elevator. She points her free hand in the direction I need to go to make it the desired room. Somehow, she already knows where her mark is and that he or she didn't evacuate the hospital regardless of all the chaos that was happening on the floor below. We make it to the intensive care unit and come up to the second door.

"Wait, Herman," Eve whispers to me. "I'll be able to walk without assistance from here," she says as she takes her arm from around me. She had already relinquished her glowing form and returned to her human state when we were in the elevator. She uses this time to get her bearings and dusts herself off. She did the best she could with her hair and wiped the blood caked on her forehead away with a clean cloth she took from the aid station just as we left the elevator. Her advanced healing powers were in full effect here, but she wasn't close to a hundred percent yet, and I could tell from her faint smile.

"We made it," I say to her as she places her hand on the doorknob and begins to twist it. "What happens from here?"

"My time here with you all is coming to an end, Herman. It has been quite the ride with you and Sean, but things will never be the same. For what it's worth, I'm happy to have you here with me for the final step. Although Sean is my protector, you aided him perfectly, and we wouldn't have made it here without you. In fact, he'll need you more than ever after all this is over," she says. She doesn't give me a chance to process or reply to her remarks as she swings the door open and steps in. I follow closely behind her. In the room is a middle-aged man and a child who is probably close to his preteen years. The man is sitting in a chair while the child is asleep on a sofa. The bedridden patient looks to be a female, judging by the anatomy. Her hair was almost completely bald, and her body is just skin and bones. She's barely holding on to life, even with the help of life support and other machines hooked up to her. The man looks up at us as we enter the room, and he rubs his eyes as if he's staring at a ghost. He stands up, slowly making his approach to Eve.

"Is that you, Krista?" He asks.

"Yes, it is, James," Eve replies. James's face lights up for a moment before his eyes revert to the woman in the bed and back to Eve.

"How is this possible, Krista? You look twenty years younger, and a little banged up, but healthy. Tell me, what's going on here? Wait, I must be dreaming."

"Yeah, Krista, please do explain what's happening here," I say to her.

"I owe you all an explanation, starting with you, James," she says as she rubs her hand across his face. "This is not a dream. I told you that I found my center before I succumbed to my illness. By centering myself, I was able to travel to the other realms. The one most notable is outer space. While we cannot travel out to it in a human state without the help of science after you center yourself, you can do such things with your consciousness, and it goes leaps and bounds beyond what science can ever uncover. I was able to find answers that supersede all answers we thought to know, such as the real reasons the world turns and how time and space are one. When I returned to my body after meditating, the answers eluded me. It was only in orbit that I could retain the information. Every star I touched in distant galaxies held a nugget of lost knowledge of those that were here before me."

"The answers to all our modern-day science questions, but what other kinds of answers are you talking about?" I query.

"ALL of them, Herman. All the unanswered questions of the universe. I wanted to retain that knowledge, so I began staying in space longer than I should – so long that my already weak body became mild nourish right under my nose. One of the stars told me of a way to exit space and bring the knowledge to Earth, but I had only mere days to reach my body."

"Your body?" I mutter as I look over at the sickly figure lying motionless on the bed. "You mean the life you came here to save wasn't just some random person; it was your own?"

She confirms it with a slow nod. "Merging with my physical body now should bring new life to it along with all I've learned from the stars. I'm not clear of what other result could come from the merger, but this is what I've come all this way for. This is what must be done."

"This is incredible," James says. "I knew you said you reached another plateau spiritually, but I didn't think what you were saying was possible. Now you stand before us, young and vibrant. If this isn't a dream and you've come after all of this, we can be a family again, and I'll never leave your side."

She gives him a weak smile and glances over at me. "The time for discussion has ended. I feel myself becoming unstable, and I must complete my connection. I'm not sure what will happen once this occurs, so I want to thank you all for being by my side during my time of need. Herman, give Sean my regards as well."

It all changed so quickly. One minute we are saving the life of a stranger and the next she's human with husband and child that have been waiting for her to come back to them. The hurt I start to feel shows how attached I've become to her. Our travels created not only an amazing, unbelievable adventure but also a love that could never be. The floor below us seem to rumble softly, snapping me back to reality, and I remember what we left on the floor below. Sean is still going at it with Felix and has no idea what is going on up here. Eve falls to one knee as her body seems to become slightly transparent, and the room feels as if the temperature is starting to rise.

"Enough of this mumbo jumbo shit, Krista. I need you to stop all this spirit talk and come back to me. Come back to us. Your son is waiting for you as well. I don't care what you must do, but he yearns to see his mother. Will you give him that at least before you go? He doesn't know you as you are now. He knows the woman he's been sitting here watching fade away day by sickening day."

"Once this is done, I will make everything right again for our family. You need only to wait another moment." Eve touches the hand of the body on the bed. A blinding light explodes from the touch itself. Even with eyes closed, all I could see was white. There was so much left to say, but I couldn't catch my breath. Time and space had already made the choice for her. Fate had already taken her away from us right from the start.

# 37.

Felix has been fighting with all his rage. Every blow he lands makes me weaker and weaker. Even though my attacks are much more effective than the last encounter we had, he is still unlike anything I've ever faced. The fight made its way into the lobby of the hospital. The chairs, vending machines, and anything that was placed here to make patients and their families feel comfortable have all been broken, torn, or used as a weapon at one point. I deliver a well-timed headbutt to his nose, stunning him as I create some distance between us to give myself a breather.

"Have you had enough, Felix? If you don't give this up soon, you're not going to like the outcome of this. You still have a chance to walk away without further damage being done," I say as I stand firm across the room from him.

"You're only fooling yourself, Hammer." Guess he acquired my name somewhere between now and when this all started. "Looks to me like you're running out of juice. I think you exerted too much energy trying to keep up with my strength, guardian, and while you have fought valiantly, you are running out of stamina. Your fight is almost over."

He' right. Being connected has given me all the power I need to fight him, but my body still hasn't fully recovered from the motel fiasco fatigue. This isn't looking good.

"I know it looks like I'm winded, but I'm just getting started. My third wind is going to kick in any minute now, and I'll end this thing. Meanwhile, Eve and Herman have more than likely done what needed to be done," I say through a smirk. "I'm having a blast showing you a thing or two, but then I didn't come here to win. I'm here to stall."

His face shows a disappointing frown. "Idiot. You choose to

sacrifice yourself for something that cannot be. That star coming here has ruined the very fabric of life in this realm and on Earth. While she has already slipped through my hands and poisoned your mind, I can still deal with you here and now, so this plaque will go no further. Fitting that this will happen here in a medical facility."

"I've had enough of this, Felix." I can feel the celestial energy within, rushing to heal all that is wrong with my body. I'm not fully healed, but there is no way I can be with this mongrel attacking me. I must attack strong, hard, and now, then find a way to escape this. I charge at him ready to give him all I got. He charges towards me preparing to do the same. When we meet in the middle, he wins by using a low, rising shoulder charge to knock the wind out of me, sending my body up into the air. I could see his body twisting to punch me midair, but there is nothing I can do to counter. The punch connects with all his momentum. I fly across the lobby and crash through a nurse's station. Sparks shoot into the air. Monitors and keyboards lie damaged and broken all around me. Blood pours down my face again, over one eye, blurring my vision. My body is aching, and I want to jump to my feet, but I can't. I can't feel the celestial energy I felt before anymore. Too injured to sustain it, my third eye vanishes. I lay here defenseless in my normal state.

"Your time is up, Hammer. You chose the wrong path to travel down, and your destiny has reached a roadblock," Felix says. I can hear his footsteps making its way towards me in no hurry, knowing that I'm too damaged to go anywhere or counter strike.

I reach into my torn jean pockets and pull out a photo. It was wrinkled and creased, and now blood smeared from my touch, but I can see them. Jasmine, whose smile is angelic, stares at me happily with our daughter, Jada, in her arms, happy as can be. Would they be proud of me now? Would they be happy to know that I didn't fight out of anger, greed, or fun, but to help someone save an innocent person's life? Or will they remember me for the monster I used to be? Living for myself and hurting all the people close to me. None of that matters now. Felix grabs me by the arm and pulls me out of the wreckage He shows no signs of weakening as he hoists me back onto my feet and raises his fist in the air. No matter how much I wanted to launch a counterattack, my body is just too thrashed to do anything, but hang there and wait for the end.

"No human can have the power that you have. Earth cannot allow such things. Unfortunately, you succumbed to the star's hoax," Felix says, showing what little pity he has for me.

I have nothing to say. I look up at his fist and wait for my demise, then suddenly he drops me. I fall to the floor with all my aches and pains holding my will hostage. Felix yells out in anger. Or is it pain? He grasps his left forearm to stop the blood from water-falling to the floor. His entire hand had been severed from his arm. Felix turns away from me with the shock of being physically injured written on top of the painful expression on his face. I follow his eyes and see a woman that looks to be Eve, but different. She's wearing a loose-fitting hospital gown. Her long dark hair blowing freely in every direction, yet there was no wind.

"Eve, what the hell are you doing here?" She says nothing, but her smile says it all; she no longer fears anything. Her third eye is gone along with the starry glow she had when assaulting her enemies, yet she illuminates a soft white light. Herman appears out of the elevator behind her with his jaw dropped.

"I was enjoying myself too much while fighting your guardian, and I let you slip through my hands," Felix says. "Just because you made it this far doesn't mean my fight is over. I can't let you or your guardian exist as long as I breathe."

Eve begins to advance towards the Gaius, her toes slightly floating above the floor as she does. "Then enjoy your last breaths of life, Felix. You have killed far too many stars but fell short of one. Let's see how you feel to be overpowered by the same thing you were created to hunt." Eve waves her hand, and Felix instantly falls flat on his face while making a blood-curdling scream. His legs from the knees down still standing upright before crumbling into piles of pebbles, dust, and blood.

"You see, Hammer? Look what you help to create. A god fueled by vengeance and power. This is all your doing and must do something to stop it," Felix pleads with me, wanting me to do something to stop his demise. Eve must have completed saving the life she was sent here to save and was granted more power for doing so. Enough power to destroy Felix without breaking a sweat and barely lifting a finger. I do nothing as I watch Eve. She approaches Felix, raises a hand to the sky that levitates what remains of Felix to her eye level. "You may destroy me now, star, but I will return. I will be reborn to save this world."

To save the world, huh? That's when things begin to add up. With Eve parading around with this power, no one would be able to stop her. She will without a doubt be a god walking among us. Did I do the right thing after all or was I fighting for the wrong side the entire time?

"AAAARRRRGHHH!"

And with that last earth rumbling cry, Félix's remains crumble to the ground of the hospital lobby along with the hopes of stopping her. Good job, Sean. You just let a distant intruder destroy the home team savior.

# 38.

"Alright, hands in the air! All of you!" a male voice shouts out to us from the other entrance of the lobby. He's decked out in tactical gear from head to toe, pointing a rifle at us as he takes slow, deliberate steps towards us. "There has been enough madness going on in here today, and we're going to have to take you all in unless you don't comply. Then we will be forced to take deadly measures." His bulletproof vest reads SWAT across the front of it. More swat members in the same attire spill into the room, making their way around us to make sure they have the perimeter surrounded. Afraid of the trouble he could get into in this encounter, Herman throws his hands and arms directly into the air and above his head.

"We're not resisting, officers, but you should listen to reason," he goes on to say as he rotates around in a semi-circle. "I know it may not look like it after all this destruction and gunfire that occurred here in the last hour, but things are now under control," he winces and places a hand over his injured mid-section. "There is no need for the hostility. The threat is over. Well, we think it is. Is it over, Eve?"

Eve's expression changes into a frown as she watches the men get in position. Her disappointment in the situation is obvious. "Listen to my friend, mortals, and put your weapons down or I will be the one forced to take action." Her brow lowers.

I'm not sure what she has planned to do to these men, but if it's anything like half of what happened to Felix, then I can't let this situation escalate any further. "Everyone, just remain calm. Officers, please listen to what I'm about to say," I shout out with my palms facing out and downward, giving them a clear view of my hands. My clothes are blood-spattered and torn half to hell, so the sight of me is enough to draw their attention, "The string of crazy events has been caused by this before you. She's nothing short of a god now. It

165

wouldn't be in any of our best interests to upset her."

"Goddess," Herman whispers to correct me.

I roll my eyes and nod. "They get the point, Herman."

"God, goddess, or streetwalker, it doesn't matter," the head officer says, signaling his men to keep their weapons trained on us with a simple head gesture. "You all have to come in with us."

"We're not going anywhere," Eve responds without delay. "Unfortunately, I can't say the same for you." A golden spark flashes across her eyes as she raises her hand slowly with her palm facing down. Her fingers are slightly bent and pointing at the swat team commander; suddenly their rifles are ripped out of their hands, merging out of reach towards the high ceiling. The weapons crack and clank as they mold into one another; chunks of metal pieces fall to the floor as the guns become one giant ball of junk metal. The men all stand, looking at the ball of guns, paralyzed with fear of what they will never understand. "Do you see now? You're wasting your time here with us. Leave now, or all of you will sacrifice your lives as the world witnesses the truth: Gods do exist," Eve states.

I can see the swat team's resolve quivering among the crowd as they all begin to back down, taking slow steps away.

"I don't know what the hell is going on here, but my orders remain the same. You're coming in with us whether you like it or not," the commander shouts as he sprints towards Eve, leaving any fear or doubt of himself behind with his men that seem to hold on to their own so well.

Eve simply says "Good" as her eyes flash again, forcefully stopping her attacker in his tracks as if something took hold of him, but there is only air in between them. It's Eve, using her power to do as she wills with him. His shined boots dangle above the polished tiled floors as he floats above it. His head looks back and forth in terror as his limbs start to pull away from one another as if they were each attached to separate invisible pulleys. "Watch closely, everyone. This is what happens when you defy a merciless god." The commander's face loses color as shock starts to set in. His teeth clench together while the stretch starts to become more painful.

A glance around the room shows everyone is frozen in fear or marvel, watching a man being slowly ripped apart by the most powerful being on the planet. For a minute I'm mesmerized by it myself like watching a terrible car accident that you can't turn away from even though you know it ends terribly. Without warning, a single set of footsteps is heard stomping against the pavement. Another officer somehow mustered up enough bravery to stop his leader's imminent death. Without Eve even flinching, a quick flash occurs, and the distinctive sound of electricity hurls the officer across the room and into a few of his other comrades. You can see the rest of the men begin to realize they are truly powerless to stop her as they start to scatter.

"I can't watch!" Herman shouts, snapping me out of my haze. Enough is enough. I close my eyes and see myself engulfed by my universe with my sun at my center. My third eye reemerges and opens, energy blasting through every facet of my body. The weakness of the battle with Felix still echoing through my bones. I must act fast. Just as the swat leader starts to scream, I rush over to Eve, tackling her in hopes of misdirecting her focus long enough to save a man's life. We slam to the ground with my body on top of hers. Her golden eyes investigate mine briefly. I can feel a faint satisfaction from her before she vanishes. My body floats in place, defying gravity as if an invisible surface is keeping me from touching the ground. I try to move, but it's impossible as if my body isn't my own. She has the same hold on me as she did on the swat commander. Eve jerks me from my hover, bringing me face to face with her. That's when I see the officer down on the tile with his limbs still intact as a member from his team rushes to aid him.

"I have no quarrel with you, Sean, and you of all people know that regardless of how powerful you have become, you are no match for me in your current state. Are you attacking me on behalf of them?" Eve's eyes look over at the people behind us before they meet with mine again, waiting for my response.

"Not just for them, but on behalf of us all," I shout, "It's my fault that you have become this being, and I'm taking responsibility for this massive mistake. I must do all I can to fix it. My life may be in shambles because of me, but I'm not going to let the world be that way because of me as well. We all have our faults, but if I can turn it all around and evolve, then the rest of the world deserves a chance to do the same."

I struggle once more to free her hold. All I can feel is the soreness against an invisible pressure. Knowing now that my chances of stopping her are null, I relax my body as I say, "Give them a chance, Eve, or you'll have to kill me to stop me." My response is direct and fierce. In my silence, I start to take in my own words and how much I've changed. Hard to believe it was me saying those words at all.

Eve shows the biggest smile I've ever seen from her. The sight of her pearly whites gives me a sensation of peace, but I'm still unsure of her intention. She grabs my head and pulls me inward to her. Her mouth close to my ear. "Never forget this feeling. You've become more than I ever dreamed you could be. Believe me when I say I am forever grateful to you. Believe in your words and sew them into your core. They will need you. I'm sorry for this, but there is no other way." She kisses my cheek before launching me through the air. I whip past the swat team and smash into the wall directly across the room, slamming into it like a wrecking ball, then falling to the floor along with chunks of bricks and mortar. My third eye closes while I hear feet rushing towards me. Without looking up from the floor, I can feel that it's Herman.

"Rejoice, for you now have been granted a new savior." Eve's voice echoes through the hospital carrying the fate of the new world in its intent. "Maybe now the people of this world will act as they should, knowing that gods do exist. I've chosen to show mercy to this planet not solely because of my friend, but because I've seen infinity and none of this measures up to the sensation of the unknown. I won't waste my energy here when there is an entire cosmos to explore like the god that was here before me."

I ease my head up from the coolness of the floor, wiping away the blood from my left eye. Eve has the attention of the entire room with all eyes on her floating silhouette. She begins to fade away.

"I'm leaving now. Before I go, I want you to witness the power of a god. We have the power to destroy and the ability to mend. Engrave my being into your eyes, soul, and your heart. Know that we are limitless, yet merciful if we chose to be." In a golden flash, she's gone. Everyone stops in their tracks, marveling at what just transpired. Meanwhile, I can feel a large amount of energy swelling inside of me. One of Eve's last gifts to me before she left, without a doubt. I can use this to get us back to Herman's truck in Tennessee. I look up at him.

Herman is just staring into the parking garage. I follow his gaze and spot Dr. Carson and his assistant from afar; happy they came back to experience this with their own eyes instead of retreating to safety. Rolling over to my side with a grunt diverts Herman's attention back to me.

"Nothing witty to say, Herm?" I ask.

"Nothing at all. I think it all speaks for itself, Sean."

The swat team leader turns to look at me, glaring as if he still wants to put me under arrest. He can save it as he points at another team member to come my way. I grab Herman's hand as my third eye opens. Just like that, we're gone, traveling in the gap between space and time.

# 39.

Herman and I pull up to the house where Jasmine lives. I could feel the sunrise as if it's somehow a part of me, revitalizing my soul with each passing second. Now that I'm not on the run or rushing about, I start to take notice of the little things that come along with being connected. The weight of the world and all the things you cared about isn't as important as the moments you live in. I always let those issues define me, but now I know the truth about it all. As the car turns off, Herman and I both look at the beautiful house in front of us and then back at each other.

"Maybe this time you won't have to choke anyone," Herman says to me jokingly, still groggy. He just woke up a few minutes before we got here.

"I can't make any promises, especially if my sister-in-law comes to the door," I reply. My injuries healed up nicely over the time it took us to get here, but it still isn't enough for me to be at a hundred percent. Nothing that a good night's rest wouldn't fix. "Herman, I want to thank you for everything you did from the beginning to now. I had a lot of weak moments during all this, and you ended up shouldering the weight I couldn't hold."

He smiles. "There was no way I could turn down a request from you, Sean. Once you proved that she was a space lady, I was sold. That and the fact you would've bashed my head in helped fuel my decision. I'm just a little disappointed about how this all turned out, you know? She had us all fooled up to the bitter end. It's like we were fighting for the wrong side the whole time."

"I understand how you feel, Herm, but let's look at this at another angle. We managed to get Eve where she needed to be, even though she had a hidden agenda. We gave her all we could give on our end,

170

but it wasn't all in vain. Look at what we've become. We pushed through the barriers within that held us back from our true selves. I mean, sure, you lacked in the muscle department, but you never gave up through all the beatings and hard times you went through with us. I think we both walked away from this knowing more about ourselves and being stronger both mentally and physically," I say, helping to ease the pain of her betrayal.

"Easy for you to say. You're the one walking away from this thing with powers," he replies as he rubs his bruised torso and winces.

"Truth be told, we all have the power in us, Herman. We all can connect to the universe inside us and be more, but we all don't play that role. That's why Eve hinged her teachings on fate. We are all connected by fate in some way or form. I don't have the answers as to why things are this way, but I will in due time. For now," I open the driver door, step out of the car, and continue speaking, "I have to see a little girl about a smile."

He nods his head in agreement as he steps out of the vehicle to stretch his legs slowly, still in pain from the soreness of all the brawling this weekend. Walking up to the driveway, I roll up the sleeves of my button-up shirt and dust off my blue jeans. It was all the clothes I found in Herman's vehicle and it beats showing up in bloodied clothing on Jasmine's doorstep like my mafia days. My time is still limited before I have to answer to what happened with all the chaos that followed me this weekend to the authorities. I also have a lot of explaining to do to these ladies inside. I ring the doorbell and wait patiently to see a familiar face peek through the curtain. The door opens almost immediately after I knock on it, and Jasmine is standing there, teary-eyed.

"Hello, Jasmine. I'm not here to cause any trouble because it's been a long weekend for both of us, but I need to see-" She interrupts me, wrapping her arms around my neck and squeezes – a feeling I've yearned for the last few months. I close my eyes in satisfaction as a wrap my arms around her, embracing her like I never have before.

"You're all over the news, Sean," she says as she lets go of me, moving to the side as to not block my view of the mounted television in the living room. Camera phone images and video of me fighting Felix in the parking garage as well as me taking down Eve inside the hospital, showing on constant rotation. The headline reads, "Suspect turned Savior?" I couldn't believe my eyes.

"I know I doubted you before, but you have to understand how unclear you were about what was going on with you. We had no idea," Jasmine says in remorse. "You have to tell me what happened out there."

"DADDY!"

Down the stairs comes my entire heart in human form –my daughter. "Jada!" My smile covers my entire face, and I drop to my knees to give her the biggest hug. She ends the hug abruptly and looks up at my forehead, tapping the center of it with her index finger.

"Where is the light you had up here like you had on the TV, dad?"

"Heh. I'll show you some other time, baby. Daddy has another issue to handle before he can relax with you." I stand to my feet as I catch Jasmine waving at Herman.

"Where is Robert, Jasmine?"

She shakes her head. "He left yesterday evening with some guys in a dark car. He said it was some pressing affairs he had to deal with alongside his legal team, but I don't know. Thanks to dealing with you in the past, my bullshit meter works better than ever."

Good. He did listen to Victor and his men after all. I'll have to deal with him personally. "I have something to say to all of you." I pause and exhale, summoning up the strength it takes to say this, "I would even like for your sister to hear this if she's around, Jazzy."

"She's not here."

Works for me. "Maybe you can pass the word along. I want you both to know that I'm different now. I know you've seen me on TV doing those incredible things, but I'm more than just those actions. I've found peace within myself, and with that, I want to give you both a peaceful life. Jasmine, you have every right not to want to be with me after what I've put you through. I want you to know that I understand and accept that, and I'll respect whatever choice you decide to make with your life as long as it's a good one."

Jasmine squeezes my hand and doesn't let it go.

"As for you, my pretty little princess, I'll always love you and protect you. Dad will always be in your heart even if I'm not able to be here all the time with you. I'll always be thinking of you, and I love you so very much."

I hug them both together, and I can feel the pressure of the past being released by the second.

"Sean! I hate to break up the family moment, but we got company," Herman shouts as he makes his way up the driveway. I step outside and see three men alongside Robert, standing on the sidewalk while Herman shuffles to the porch, almost ignoring all his pain to get away from the danger to come.

"I know what you did to Victor, Hammer. This doesn't change anything. You are not supposed to be here, but because you were stupid enough to come back even after what you did, you're going to feel the consequences by any means necessary," Robert says as his points a finger towards the entire household.

"You saved me the time of going to find you, and I thank you for that, but now I'm going to have to treat you like every other man that decided to use my family against me."

Jasmine frowns. "Sean, what the hell is he talking about? How do I end up attracting all the bad guys?"

"Herm, please take Jasmine and Jada in the house for a minute," I request before a big grin shoots across my face as I wink at him. "This will only take a second."

"The fun never ends when you're around, does it?" Herman says, following my directive. The door closes behind them, leaving me alone to face the aggressors.

Robert points at me and signals his crew to get me. The celestial energy begins pulsing through me again, and my third eye opens, stopping them in their tracks on their approach. You can see the fear of the unknown beginning to hit them like a sucker punch.

"I've been here before, but never like this."

# 40.

Examining the sky above, I can see debris floating around just outside the atmosphere of my newly stabilized planet. My sun shines down far above the deep blue sky. Small blazes of twinkling lights can be seen dancing in the atmosphere like glitter shining from different angles as I walk along the grassy plains. Mountains high enough to have snow on top of their peaks can be seen in the distance of it all. Nothing can describe the sensation of merely breathing in the air.

"This is your new home," Eve's voice says clearly, no longer carrying the faint echo it had during the connection process. Facing her, she is no longer transparent, but a split image of her physical self. Not in her god state, but in her star form. All three eyes are open with her glowing skin gleaming like the stars in the distance, yet closer. "Do you know what I'm doing here?"

My instinct kicks in, answering the question, "You're here to close our link."

"That's right. I'm in this state because I was in this form when I set up this endpoint while you were recovering from your first assault on Felix, therefore any event that took place after is somewhat a mystery to me for my memory only goes up to that point of my creation. I'm not sure what happened out there in the world after that night, but I see you've managed to survive and create a whole new world for yourself. One with life and stability that you longed for all these years. From here you can travel the cosmos, learn and see things you can never imagine, but they can't leave this plain. Nothing can harm you here but be wary of this state. Staying here too long can cause you to neglect everything else. A part of me misses the life I had as a human being, but judging how well things went here, I must have moved on with my plans."

"That you did, Eve. You used us to reach godliness and dipped out of our lives just as swiftly as you came into it. I am grateful though. I cherish everything so much more since my Universing." I frown immediately after saying it.

"Universing?" Eve questions.

"A new word, courtesy of Herman. He likes the term better than Connecting."

"I think I like it, Sean."

I scoff before walking over to her and place my hand on her shoulder. "So, this it then? Once you leave, our link will be closed, and you'll be just a memory, right?"

"Yeah, that's right. You'll probably never see me again, but always remember all the things I've taught you. With me gone, you're free to do as you please with the world. I can only assume we defeated Felix, but the Earth will give birth to a new Gaius soon, and the Gaius will seek you out when the time comes, especially if you are using your powers just as I was. Until then, you are free to do as you please. You can even guide others to reach their star in the universe. It's all up to you. I know my actions may have seemed a bit selfish in the end, but at least I left you awakened in place of the Gaius."

"That's why you couldn't let me die. You knew that if we were to complete your journey, there would be no one here to protect the world from the next fallen star that might not have your tact. You do care about the world in your own twisted way." I pull her to me and squeeze her tightly. She wraps her arms around me tight at first, but her grip loosens as she starts to fade away.

"Goodbye, Sean."

"Thank you and goodbye, Eve."

Her existence floats upward and becomes twinkling dust, mixing in with the tiny sparkles already in the air. I look up into the great blue sky and see distant planets. Now that she's truly gone, I can feel the universe becoming a part of me as I stand on this great plain of peace and serenity. This moment is the calmest I have ever felt. I remember that all the answers to it all are beyond that sky, on those planets. Maybe one day I'll care to know them, but for now, I'm happier just knowing my family loves me again. That's enough for me.

~End~

# EPILOGUE

Finally arriving at Dr. Carson's home, I step out of my car, making my way down the driveway to the steps of his porch. The doctor always loved his privacy, and it shows in the placement of his home. He had acres of land that were left untended the last time I was here, but it looks like he's been keeping himself busy since the events at the hospital two weeks ago. He took leave the morning after Eve left and days later, he put in his resignation. They promoted me to his position, but I couldn't get in touch with him via phone or email which is why I'm here now. I knock on his brown, paint-chipped wooden door. It swings open with little to no effort on my part. Pine scents and polish fumes emit faintly from inside. The foyer appears cleaner than I've ever seen it. So clean that I had to peek outside to make sure I'm barging into the right home with a glance at the outside of the porch and a shorter glance at his parked van.

"Come on back, Samuel. I figured you would be showing up here eventually, my former apprentice!" Dr. Carson yells from the office in the back down the hall. For a moment, I wonder how he knows it was me, but he and I both know that I'm the only one that ever comes to visit him these days.

"Good to hear your voice, Dr. Carson. I was afraid I'd entered the wrong house seeing how clean your things are. What's the occasion?" I ask, strolling down the hallway, stepping lightly on his hardwood floors in my dress shoes so as not to scuff it.

"I think we have quite a few things to celebrate, Sam," he shouts in response. "You've been promoted to my old position, once considered a place for one's career to be ended and now made into a full-blown sister agency of its own in light of recent events."

He speaks the truth. His knowledge of human behavior has yet to amaze me, but what I see next does. The office has been totally broken down. There are no papers to sift through to find a proper sitting spot or empty styrofoam trays to stuff into an already filled trash bin. Everything is spotless down to the rug on the floor – a rug that I never

177

noticed until this very moment. It has long lost its fluff, but it was stainless. The doctor himself is also in rare form; he's dressed down in sweats and an old college red t-shirt with the mascot mostly faded. He hasn't bothered to shave. His 5'oclock shadow is way past midnight. He's standing at the pinboard, taking down the last few images of Felix that we were researching weeks ago when I was last here.

Stunned by his appearance, I say, "Quite the transformation, Dr. Carson. Not just for the office, but you as well. These past two weeks away from the labs have put some spunk in your life, I see." It has done more than that. His face even looks less stressed. "I see you're moving on to your next research project."

He nodded in disagreement. "Not exactly, Samuel. All the cleaning I've done is as a result of my depression. You have to understand that once Eve revealed her true self to us, it proved that science is no longer relevant. That there are people that defy those rules that we hinged all our research upon, and it turns out it was all in jest.

It was another surprise to hear him say, but I can't argue with his reasoning. Now I can see why he would be so depressed. All his hard efforts of higher learning for over a decade on top of self- teaching years in his field of studies, gone to waste in his eyes. Witnessing Eve in her goddess state has left an everlasting impression on the world; especially in his world. "Are you just going to toss out all the work and research you compiled over all these years? I know her appearance changes things, but that doesn't make science irrelevant, Doctor Carson. We still can make strides in the world with the help of others like you, willing to dedicate themselves to this calling of ours. Don't be so hard on yourself."

He turns and faces me with a smile as he replies. "You make a valid argument, Samuel, but none of those advancements have anything to do with my previous field of study. I'm not counting out all science, but anything that says we don't have a soul is so far from correct. Our run-in with Felix and the others speaks volumes on the matter," he says as he hands me the stack of pictures and looks back at the muted television. The headline reads, "Another crisis averted," as the reporter stands next to Sean, getting a statement on his heroic actions. He went into hiding for a week and came back at full force, showing up around the world as they need him. "My hypothesis is that Felix wasn't just a protector of the planet, but the breathing embodiment of the Earth. It explains why he never aged all these years and why his powers were Earth-based," the doctor says, bringing back the topic at hand.

"That's a bold observation, but I don't count anything out these days after seeing Sean do what he does now. The thing about your theory is that it's difficult to prove it to be true. No form of science can test the soul of any being," I respond, flipping through the images of Felix NASA's cameras has captured over the years. "How do you plan on making your claims a reality?"

"I'm happy you asked, Samuel. While it would be impossible to make formulas and equations to prove it, I've been doing some research on the matter on my own," he says as he begins to exit the room, signaling me to follow. "I took all the information you put in the debrief as well as the things I've been studying to learn how to test my theory. Sean was able to dive deep into his consciousness and master his soul. His pineal gland or third eye was able to open, and he ascended to a whole new level of human capabilities. This alone defies any study of science we have yet to witness, thus making it impossible to get the answers we seek."

I follow him into another room down a small side hallway. The room itself was dimly lit by candlelight, void of any desk or furniture. The windows are covered with thick black curtains to block out any natural light. The candles are placed in a circle around a square, plush maroon rug. I start to contemplate his angle with such a dramatic setup. His hand grips my bicep firmly. My eyes dart to his grip and then directly to his eyes, filled with what I can only describe as anticipation.

"The only way to comprehend what happened at that hospital; the only way to learn how Eve and Sean were able to become awakened, Samuel, is to recreate it. The only way to do that is beyond our primitive studies. The only way to do what they were able to do is to master your consciousness with-"

In an instant, I realize what he's hinting at and we both say the word in cadence.

"Meditation."

# FINAL NOTE

Now that the story is over, I hope I was able to spark something in your imagination. Not just that, but I also hope my work proves that even a full-time worker, part-time soldier, and single father of two can strive and make his dreams of publishing a book a reality somehow. Don't be afraid to go for your dreams no matter what situation you may find yourself in. Let it be known that it is NEVER too late to stride. Thank you from the bottom of my heart for reading and you'll be hearing from me again, soon.

~Trey Persons~

# ABOUT THE AUTHOR

## TREY PERSONS

Trey Persons is an Operation Iraqi Freedom veteran/writer with a deep love for fantasy and poetry. He wrote his debut novel, UNIVERSING, while working a nine to five, still serving the country as an Army National Guardsman, and raising his two toddler sons. He hopes that pursuing his dreams to become a published author despite his situation will inspire others to achieve their goals and heart's desires. Trey resides in Memphis, Tennessee where you can find him playing video games, raising his two sons, and writing future novels. Contact info is below.

Blog: https://writeofmight.com/

Instagram: https://www.instagram.com/treypersons/

Twitter: https://twitter.com/PersonsTrey

Email: authortreypersons@gmail.com

Made in the USA
Coppell, TX
05 August 2020